'Not all women irresistible.'

'Is that what I believe

'Do you actually deny it?' She threw the challenge at him with unconcealed irritation— though the irritation she felt was with herself as much as him. Why was she pursuing this dangerously loaded conversation? Why didn't she simply put an end to it?

But she didn't. Instead, she added, 'You've always believed it. You've always believed no woman could resist you.'

Dear Reader

This month, I would like to ask you to think about the kind of heroine you would like to find in our stories. Do you think she should be sweet and gentle, on the look-out for a man who will be able to care for and nurture her, or should the heroine be able to give as good as she gets, throwing punch for punch, and quite capable of standing up for herself? If you have any opinions on this matter please let us know, so that we can continue to give you the books you want to read!

The Editor

Stephanie Howard was born and brought up in Dundee in Scotland, and educated at the London School of Economics. For ten years she worked as a journalist in London on a variety of women's magazines, among them *Woman's Own*, and was latterly editor of the now defunct *Honey*. She has spent many years living and working abroad—in Italy, Malaysia, the Philippines and in the Middle East. Currently, she lives in Kent.

Recent titles by the same author:

LOVE'S VENDETTA
DANGEROUS INHERITANCE
NO GOING BACK
THE PHARAOH'S KISS

COUNTERFEIT LOVE

BY
STEPHANIE HOWARD

MILLS & BOON LIMITED
ETON HOUSE, 18-24 PARADISE ROAD
RICHMOND, SURREY TW9 1SR

First published in Great Britain 1993
by Mills & Boon Limited

© Stephanie Howard 1993

Australian copyright 1993
Philippine copyright 1993
This edition 1993

ISBN 0 263 78174 7

Set in Times Roman 11 on 12 pt.
01-9308-48183 C

Made and printed in Great Britain

CHAPTER ONE

SALLY was posting a letter at the corner postbox when suddenly she was struck by lightning.

At least, she reflected later, that was what it had felt like when she'd glanced up with a start to find Josh standing in front of her. It was as though a lightning bolt had struck her squarely in the forehead, shot right through her body then exited through her feet.

Shell-shocked, she blinked up at the tall, dark figure, all wild black hair and piercing jet eyes, broad shoulders tautening the lines of his shirt, his hands stuffed lazily into the pockets of his trousers. And she shivered, feeling the blood turn to ice in her veins and the hairs on the back of her neck stand on end.

But then she gathered herself together instantly. 'My!' she said, looking at him. 'I wonder what I've done to deserve this?'

'I wonder, indeed.'

He was leaning casually against the postbox, a portrait of glittering, virile male arrogance, smiling at her with that smile she knew so well and hated. The smile of a man who knew he owned the world.

Sally resisted the urge to reach up and smooth her hair or check that her blouse buttons were all properly done up. And the fact that she could resist was a small, pleasing triumph. For, once, she would not have been able to resist. Once, she would have

5

succumbed to the unease he evoked in her, overcome by that sensation of defensive vulnerability that, even now, she could remember all too well.

But though her unease spurted inside her she was able to douse it quickly. She knew he looked down on her, but she no longer cared.

He was looking down on her now—in a more literal fashion!—that mocking arrogant smile of his still playing around his lips. 'I've been looking for you,' he informed her, his eyes skimming over her, taking in the short blonde hair and neat svelte figure, dressed in a simple blouse and skirt. 'I was told that you were out on business. I was on my way home when I suddenly caught sight of you.'

He leaned more comfortably against the postbox. 'Wasn't that a bit of luck?'

'An incredible bit of luck.'

Sally grimaced inwardly and fought to quell her sudden alarm. It was—how long since their last meeting? All of eighteen months. These days Josh rarely came to the village—his international business was based in London. And that last meeting had been fleeting and barely civil, just like all their other meetings over the previous decade. If he had come looking for her now, it could mean only one thing—trouble. When Josh stepped into her life, it always meant trouble.

He was smiling at her, knowing precisely what she was thinking. Sally sensed his amusement as he said, 'Yes, that's what I thought, too. An incredible bit of luck.' The dark eyes danced at her with uncaring arrogance. 'There I was, driving back to Aunt Mimi's, resigned to the fact that you were nowhere to be found, when suddenly I caught sight of you crossing the road, on your way to post a letter. Quite frankly, I couldn't have been more delighted.'

'How unusual.' Sally regarded him through sceptical sea-green eyes. 'You're not usually so delighted to see me.'

'Aren't I?'

'Definitely not.'

Josh smiled. 'You could be right.' His dark eyes narrowed behind the long sooty lashes. 'I guess I was so delighted because it saved me having to look for you. You know how much I hate to waste time.'

That was more like it. Sally nodded with understanding. Josh had always been a man in a hurry. Even when he was very young she had sensed his impatience. She had known he would scale great heights, and quickly.

It was that boundless energy of his that she found both invigorating and overwhelming. It radiated from him even now, like sparks of electricity, as he leaned, apparently casually, against the postbox. Reach out to touch him and he'd make your flesh jump!

She doused the unexpected flare that thought aroused in her and concentrated carefully on her sense of antipathy. 'What a pity, then,' she said, 'that I popped up so conveniently for you. I rather like the idea of you having to search for me.'

'I'll bet you do.' Josh caught her eye and held it. 'I'll bet you'd also have preferred it if I hadn't found you.'

That claim, as they both knew, needed no verbal affirmation. Sally's normally soft green eyes regarded him stonily, taking in the strong tanned planes of his face, the glossy dark hair, the glittering jet-black eyes, and felt the sense of alarm within her double.

He was as handsome as ever, she found herself thinking. If he were anyone but Josh, just the sight of him would melt her. It would be a pleasure just to look into his face.

But he *was* Josh, so how could she do anything other than wish with all her heart that he'd never found her, when all he'd ever brought her was suffering and shame?

'So, aren't you going to post your letter?'

As he spoke, Sally started and glanced down at the letter that she'd forgotten all about and still held in her hand.

Josh added, 'I take it that was your intention?'

'Yes, that was my intention.' Sally pulled herself together and with a flourish pushed the letter through the mouth of the postbox. 'There!' she pronounced, as it plopped inside. If only she could just turn around and go now, she was thinking!

Faint hope! Josh was obviously far from finished with her. As though held by invisible strings, she faced him and demanded, not at all sure she wanted to hear the answer, 'So, for what particular reason were you looking for me?'

'Perhaps just to say hello.'

'Oh, yes, I'd believe that!' Sally tossed her blonde head. 'I see you haven't lost your sense of humour.' Then she made a pretence at turning to leave. 'In that case,' she parried, 'since you've said hello, it will now be my pleasure to say goodbye!'

He stopped her, as she had known he would, without even touching her. He simply shifted slightly, blocking her path.

'If only it were so simple, it would be more pleasant for both of us.' Josh frowned. 'But, alas, there's more to it than that.'

'I suspected there would be.' Sally's heart shrank within her. As he'd moved, he'd straightened, so that his tall, powerful frame all at once was towering over her. Suddenly, he seemed very dark and threatening.

The black eyes glinted down at her, and they were faintly threatening too. There was barely a trace now of his previous arrogant amusement.

'So what do you want with me?' Sally added, hiding her nervousness.

'Not here.' Josh straightened further. 'My place or yours. Take your pick. I'm easy,' he told her.

Easy? That was funny! Josh was many things, but never in his life could he have been described as easy!

But Sally didn't comment. Instead, as casually as she could manage, she demanded, 'Does it have to be right now?'

'It doesn't have to be. It can be this evening, if you prefer.' The dark eyes flicked over her. 'Why, are you busy?'

'A bit.' Her mind was churning. Would it be better to postpone it? Or, whatever it was, should she get it over with now?

Josh smiled again. 'You choose the time. See how accommodating I am? I'm easy about that, too.'

He was mocking her. That was obvious. He had picked up her nervousness and it would amuse him, Sally suspected, to spin out her agony.

That was why she decided, 'OK, let's make it now.'

I won't play his little game, she thought. I won't let him manipulate me. And besides, she had no reason to be nervous. He had no holds on her. No influence in her life.

'We can talk at the shop,' she added in a firm tone. 'I was on my way there anyway, as it happens.'

'Sounds good to me. Let's meet up at the shop, then.' Josh turned and waved to where his car was parked, across the street, right behind her little van. 'I'll see you there in about five minutes.'

'Five minutes. OK.' Sally nodded in agreement as, with a final glance at her, he headed for his car, a bright red, fearsomely ferocious-looking Italian job that somehow perfectly reflected the character of its owner. And, though her step was firm as she strode across the road behind him, suddenly Sally's heart felt heavy inside her.

What did he want with her? She prayed it was something simple. Something that could be dealt with with the minimum of disruption.

And how could it be anything else? she reassured herself hurriedly. These days, their lives were totally separate. And her life—the shop, her painting and Clive—was securely beyond Josh's destructive reach. There was no possible harm that he could do her.

But as she climbed behind the driver's wheel and glanced in her mirror quickly, as the red Ferrari growled into life, she knew deep in her heart that she was fooling herself. She had always had trouble staying out of Josh's reach. And he had never had any trouble inflicting harm.

And as he seemed to meet her eyes in the mirror and smiled, fear settled like a stone in the pit of her stomach. Every single aspect of her life, she suspected, was about to be turned ruthlessly upside-down.

By the time she reached the shop Sally had pulled herself together.

She had watched the mean-looking red Ferrari disappear ahead of her down the dusty road, lined on either side by summer-green sycamores, and in a firm voice had recited a couple of home truths to herself.

Number one: Josh Kingsley was an egotistical bastard whom she ought to have more sense than to allow to upset her. Surely she had grown out of such vulnerability long ago?

And number two: in spite of his trouble-making nature, there was no reason to fear that he could make trouble for her. She had simply been silly to imagine that he could.

It was that contempt which she could sense in him, and the way he could look at her, that still had the power to awaken irrational fears.

She drew up outside the shop that was set back from the road a little, right in the heart of the pretty Kentish village where she had happily spent most of her twenty-four years. And, as always, in spite of the red Ferrari that was now parked there and the tall, dark figure who was standing in the doorway, she felt a warm, reassuring glow of achievement.

This was hers. Hers and Clive's. This chic little arts and crafts shop with its painted wooden sign, bearing the proud legend 'The Treasure Trove' was proof, if proof had ever been needed, that, in spite of Josh's low opinion of her, she amounted to something worthwhile in the world. From nothing—and with Clive's invaluable assistance, of course—she'd built up a flourishing little business.

On that spine-straightening thought, Sally stepped from the van, suddenly not caring a jot why Josh wished to see her.

'I have some pictures I have to unload from the van.' She tossed him a quick glance as she strode to the back of the van, pulled open the doors and leaned inside. Then, to annoy him, she added, 'It'll only take a few minutes.' He would be expecting her to make herself instantly available. That was the kind of submissive behaviour Josh liked.

He also, of course, enjoyed being in charge.

'I'll take them for you.' All at once he was right behind her, one hand extended. 'They look as though they're heavy.'

'They're not particularly heavy. I can manage.' Sally shot him an annoyed glance over her shoulder as she lifted the framed pictures to the mouth of the van. 'I do this sort of thing all the time.'

'Doesn't that boyfriend of yours help you, then?' He hadn't budged a centimetre, and clearly had no intention of doing so until she handed him the pictures. And that was so typical of Josh, thought Sally. He liked his own way.

He added, eyeing her, 'I'm surprised. I thought by now you'd have him better trained.'

'Better trained?' Sally laughed and lifted one curved eyebrow. 'Don't tell me you think it's a woman's place to try and train the men in her life? Men aren't dogs or horses, you know. They're supposed to be responsible adults.'

'And some of us are.' Josh smiled back at her in amusement. 'Yet some women regard it as a kind of vocation to try and change the men in their lives. And, of course, some men are actually fool enough to let them do it.'

'But not you, of course?'

'That goes without saying.'

Sally had to smile. Yes, it did go without saying. She had seen with her own eyes how immune he was to the reforming zeal of his countless girlfriends.

But as he caught her smile and smiled back at her amusedly, Sally snatched her gaze away as a strange sensation shot through her.

Well, not strange, quite familiar, really, though it had belonged in the past, that vulnerable clutching sensation at her heart as their eyes had met and that smile had passed between them.

She pushed it away now and suddenly found herself wishing that he wasn't boxing her in quite so tightly against the back of the van. His hard, virile body seemed to imprison her.

She said, forcing a light tone, still holding on to the pictures, 'Well, I'm not that reforming type of woman, anyway. And fortunately Clive doesn't need to be trained.'

'I see. He's perfect, is he?'

'Oh, I don't think anyone's perfect.' She met his eyes in challenge. 'Do you?' she countered.

'I believe all things are possible.' He met her challenge with a smile. Dark eyes glanced down at her as he tilted his head arrogantly. 'And, since I believe that, I suppose I have to believe that there's a scattering of perfect individuals in the world.'

'And I suppose you also believe you know where at least one of them is scattered?' Sally's tone was mocking and tight with disapproval. She had known for years that Josh believed himself perfect!

'I know this much . . .' He leaned against the van door, causing Sally's heart to rush within her as he seemed to box her in even more. 'I know that, wherever they're scattered, there are none of them in your life . . . I'm referring to your dear boyfriend, of course. He definitely isn't one of them.'

That was rich! 'You don't even know him!'

'I've had the displeasure of his acquaintance.'

'Once! For two minutes!'

'Two minutes were quite enough.'

As he paused, Sally was wishing he would move out of the way. He was standing so close now, she could smell the warm scent of him and could feel, almost like a warm hand pressed against her, the muscular power of his body. And the more aware she became of these things, the harder she was finding it to breathe.

He seemed oblivious of her discomfort. His black eyes mocked her as he elaborated, 'As I said, two minutes were quite enough. I'm a swift—and very accurate—judge of character.'

As he said it, he smiled a light, amused smile, but at the back of the black eyes a dark shadow had fallen. And that look, without the need for any words, was enough to remind Sally of how he had judged *her*—and of how that judgement, and the unfairness of it, had nearly crippled her.

Renewed anger poured through her. She no longer felt his prisoner. Hadn't she ceased to be Josh's prisoner long ago?

She thrust the pictures at him. 'If you're so keen to help, take them!' Then she was stepping past him, breathing deeply, heading swiftly for the door of the shop.

'Hi, Sharon. How's it been? Any customers?'

Sally smiled at the young girl who was seated behind the counter and felt her tension flow away. She was on her own turf now. Here Josh was the stranger. Here he no longer had any power over her.

Sharon had grown pink. She was rising to her feet. 'I sold one of those little jewel boxes, but that's all, I'm afraid.'

'One of the shell jewel boxes? Good for you.' Sally was smiling at Sharon, but Sharon's eyes were elsewhere. They were fixed like two eager blue limpets on Josh.

'Hello, Sharon.' And, of course, Josh responded. Didn't he always respond to the blushing overtures of women? 'So, you're working for Sally these days?'

'Only part-time...until I can find a full-time job. I left school, you see, at the end of last term.'

As she spoke, poor Sharon had grown even pinker. Sally could almost hear the confused beating of her heart. She sighed to herself resignedly, reflecting with mild annoyance that she'd seen this little scene enacted a thousand times with a thousand different girls. Once, she had even been one of them herself. Unfailingly, Josh had this effect on females.

Until one learns to see behind the seductive, handsome mask, she reminded herself. Then, happily, one becomes immune.

'You can go now, if you want. I'm going to shut up soon, and I doubt there'll be any more customers today.' Sally addressed the still wide-eyed, pink-cheeked Sharon, though she suspected the poor girl hadn't heard a single word. So, smiling fondly, she repeated herself, this time a little louder. 'You can go home now, Sharon, if you like.'

'Oh?' Sharon had heard her. She glanced round at Sally, blinking. 'Don't you want me to give you a hand with these pictures?'

'Don't worry, Sharon. I'll help Sally.' Josh had spoken. 'There's no need for you to hang about.'

'Oh? OK. Thanks.' Sharon gathered herself together. She reached for her bag beneath the counter. 'I'll see you both later, then,' she said, and hurried off.

'So where do you want the pictures?'

As the door closed behind Sharon, Josh turned to Sally, one dark eyebrow lifted. And there was a look of such cool detachment in the dark eyes that one might almost have believed he was totally unaware of the havoc he'd just caused in Sharon's heart. He always gave that impression: that he neither knew nor cared much about the power he had over women.

Which was pretty smart, it had always occurred to Sally. It simply made it even easier for him to exploit that power.

She met his gaze with a cool look. 'I'll take them through to the store-room.' She held out her arms to take the paintings.

But he did not hand them over. He simply smiled back at her with that amused, faintly arrogant smile she so hated. 'I'll take them,' he told her. 'I believe in finishing the jobs I start. I wouldn't dream of abandoning this one halfway.'

Sally shrugged. 'Suit yourself. The store-room's over there.'

She crossed to a door and pushed it open. Then she stepped aside smartly to let him pass through. She wasn't going to make the same mistake she'd made at the van and end up imprisoned with him in the store-room!

Switching on the light, she told him, 'Just put them anywhere. Stack them singly against the wall.'

As he proceeded to do so, Sally stood in the doorway and watched him. It was no wonder, she found herself thinking, that he affected women the way he did. With his dark good looks and muscular physique he was, frankly, the best-looking man she'd ever seen. But his good looks were only a small part of his power. It was another, less tangible quality in him that caused female hearts to wilt.

She narrowed her sea-green eyes at him as he stacked the pictures against the wall. It was the air of untameable wildness he had about him, faintly threatening, but at the same time wholly exciting.

Danger sprang from him. It crackled in the air around him. And women were drawn to him like moths to a flame.

'Some of these are rather good.'

As he straightened and spoke suddenly, Sally was jolted out of her reverie. She blinked at him in confusion. 'Sorry, what did you say?'

'I said some of these paintings are rather good. Is the artist someone local?'

'Yes, he lives locally. Down by the Old Mill. We've sold a fair bit of his work. He's pretty popular.'

'I'm not surprised. I wouldn't mind one myself.' Josh was walking back across the store-room towards her. In the doorway he paused. 'And how about you? Are you doing any painting these days?'

'A bit. When I have time.' Sally felt reluctant to discuss with him this essential, vital part of her life. For the truth was, she painted whenever she could. Her painting was more important to her than anything else.

She shrugged. 'The shop takes up most of my time.'

'Yes, I expect it does.' Josh was watching her closely. There was an oddly calculating look in his eye. 'So tell me,' he put to her, gesturing behind him to the paintings he had just finished stacking in the store-room, 'what kind of prices do you sell these for?'

Sally thought for a moment. 'It depends on the size and the subject matter. Some are more popular than others.'

'I imagine the landscapes are most popular.' Josh stepped through the doorway to stand before her and suddenly there was an oddly predatory glint in his eye. 'Just from that small selection there, I'd say landscapes were his strong point.'

'Yes, you're right, they tend to be most popular.'

Sally wanted to move away, but suddenly she couldn't. She felt as though her feet were nailed to the floor. And it was that dark predatory look in his eyes that had nailed them there.

She added a little huskily, 'Everybody likes them.'

'I'll bet they do.'

He felt uncomfortably close now, though he was standing a good couple of feet away. It was the way he was looking at her, seeming to drain the strength from her, making her his prisoner with his eyes.

He said, 'Do you sell them locally or do you have contacts nationwide?'

'Locally, mostly. Just like most of our merchandise.'

As she looked back at him, Sally felt her heart tighten uncomfortably. Perhaps these were just casual questions he was asking, but for some reason, increasingly, they were beginning to feel like an inquisition.

She took a deep breath and, overcoming that feeling, elaborated, 'We have one or two customers who've bought from us while they were on holiday. Occasionally I contact one of them if I have something I think they'd like.'

'So not everything is bought locally?'

'No, but most of it is.'

'Most of it . . . meaning the more run-of-the-mill stuff?'

'No, I didn't mean that. None of our stuff's run-of-the-mill. All our artists and craftspeople are highly talented.' Sally felt a flare of protective anger at his insult. The men and women whose work she sold she considered almost as family!

Josh smiled cynically at her loyalty. 'Yes, but some are more talented than others. The work of some of them—like that artist whose work I've just delivered to the store-room—could be sold elsewhere at far higher prices than you could ever demand locally. I mean, in London, for example, you could probably charge double.'

Sally looked back at him, feeling the tightness within her become tighter. This was definitely turning into an inquisition!

A little impatiently she told him, 'I run a crafts shop in Kent and I charge the sort of prices that are appropriate for the area. I don't know anything about the market in London...'

'Don't you?' All at once, he had reached out one hand towards her and caught her lightly around the jaw with his long tanned fingers. The fingers seemed to hold her there. His eyes burned like hot irons. 'Forgive me, but I find that a little difficult to believe.'

For a moment Sally froze at the cool touch of the long fingers. She felt her heart break into a nervous gallop. Then, as he thrust his face closer, her limbs were momentarily paralysed. She stared at him, blinking foolishly, as he growled, 'You're lying, aren't you?'

'Lying?' What had got into him? Had he gone crazy or something? 'Why would I be lying?'

'Because of your dishonest nature.' His eyes glinted down at her. 'You never did find honesty very easy.'

Sudden anger poured through Sally, and with it the will to defend herself. With her fist she punched the hand that held her prisoner—though it struck her that, really, he was holding her so lightly all she need have done was snatch her face away.

'Let go of me!' she yelled. 'How dare you lay a hand on me?'

Josh smiled contemptuously, dropping his hand away. 'You're right, I shouldn't have done that. One never knows... Dishonesty like yours might be contagious.'

Sally felt her face stiffen as, dry-mouthed, she looked back at him. His words and his expression of total contempt for her were deeply shocking, though she knew they shouldn't be. Why should she care that he continued to hold such a low opinion of her?

And she didn't care, she told herself. She was simply taken aback that he should throw in her face that regrettable incident that had formed his low opinion of her all these years ago. That incident, by now, ought to be water under the bridge.

But, from the way he was looking at her, that was far from being the case. As she stepped away from him, her legs like straw beneath her, he observed in a harsh tone, 'What a little liar you are!'

Sally swung round on him then. She did not have to put up with this. Between clenched teeth, she told him, 'You said you wanted to speak to me. That's the only reason I allowed you to set foot inside my shop.' She paused by the counter and leaned gratefully against it. 'Whatever it is you want to talk about, I'd be grateful if you'd just get on with it.'

'Oh, don't worry, I'm getting there.' His arms were folded across his chest as Josh continued to stand in the store-room doorway. 'I won't keep you waiting very much longer.'

'I'd prefer it if you didn't keep me waiting at all. I have better things to do than hang around listening to you.'

'I doubt it. I think you'll find that listening to me, though perhaps not pleasurable, will prove to be highly informative.'

'And what is that supposed to mean?' Sally's fingers gripped the counter. She was beginning to feel like a mouse in a trap.

'All in good time.' Josh fixed her with a look that warned her it would be a waste of time to try to hurry him. But she knew that already. He would do things his way, just as he had always done all his life.

He reached behind him and pulled the store-room door closed. Then he narrowed his eyes at her. 'Perhaps you ought to lock it. I'm sure you wouldn't like some other thief breaking in and walking off with all your profits.'

Some other thief. No, he hadn't forgotten. Guiltily, remembering, Sally dropped her gaze away. But he was wrong: though she had acted like one, she had never been a thief. But there was no point in telling him that now, just as there hadn't been then.

She said, keeping her tone level, forcing her eyes to meet his again, 'Don't worry, I'll lock up everything before I go.' She was about to add, Which will be just as soon as you've said what you have to say. But she stopped herself in time. That would only make him take longer!

Josh had stepped away from the door now and was glancing round the shop, at the shelves of glass and pottery and wood carvings. Flicking her a glance, he observed, 'You have quite an impressive selection of stuff here. I see that not everything, after all, gets shipped up to London.'

Why was he keeping on about London? Was he trying to confuse her?

Deliberately, Sally ignored the allusion. 'Yes,' she responded in a crisp tone, 'we have a lot of nice things.'

'Very nice. I congratulate you on your taste.' He smiled a blatantly condescending smile. 'But then in such matters you always did show good taste.'

She had a memory of long ago when she was still a child and he, seven years older, was not much more than one himself. He'd said something similar to her then, that she had an eye for beautiful things. She could remember even now how pleased and flattered she'd felt.

But eighteen years had passed and she was no longer a six-year-old child and Josh no longer had the power either to please or to flatter her.

She responded in a scathing tone. 'You mean it coincides with yours? That's what people generally mean when they say someone has good taste.'

'Is it?' He neither accepted nor rejected her judgement. More than likely, he considered it did not apply to him. As they both knew, the things that other people did or said were not necessarily the sorts of things that Josh did and said. No one could ever have accused him of running with the herd.

He continued to study with apparent interest the little shop and its contents. 'You must have worked pretty hard to build this place up. When Aunt Mimi rented the shop out to you it had been standing empty for years. And now look at it. Quite a transformation.'

'Yes, we've worked hard.' It had been eighteen months of constant slog! But every ounce of effort had been worth it. She now had the means to support herself, and her painting.

'Yes, you must have worked hard... You and... what's his name.'

As he spoke, Josh had picked up a delicate china pot that had been standing on the display unit by the window. He weighed it in his hand as Sally answered, 'His name's Clive.'

'Ah, yes, of course... Clive.' He smiled amusedly. He found it entertaining to subtly insult her by pretending to forget the name of her partner and boyfriend. He glanced down at the delicate pot, then back to Sally again. 'So, where is... Clive? Why isn't he here?'

'He's away on business... seeing some of our craftspeople. Why? Did you particularly want to see him?'

Josh shook his head. 'No, not particularly. I was thinking rather that he might wish to be here. As he's your partner in the business, I'm sure he'd be interested in what I have to tell you...'

As he spoke, he tossed the pot lightly in the air.

Sally felt a dart of double anxiety. Anxiety at the ominous note in his voice, and anxiety at his cavalier handling of the pot. It was a particularly lovely piece and one she virtually had a buyer for.

Her eyes glued to the pot, she responded, 'And what have you come to tell me?' Suddenly, she dared not look into his eyes.

Again he tossed the pot and caught it lightly. Without compassion, he said, 'Bad news, I'm afraid.'

'Bad news? What do you mean?' As fear jerked inside her, Sally shifted her gaze once more to mesh with his. 'What are you talking about? What kind of bad news?'

'The worst, I'm sorry to say.' He tossed the pot again. Sally followed his movements as he caught it deftly in his hand. 'All this...' With his free hand he gestured around him. 'All this, alas, is about to end.'

'End?' She felt a coldness start at her feet and slowly travel up to her scalp. She didn't know what he was talking about, but she could tell he wasn't joking.

'Yes, end.' His eyes were on her, cold and merciless. 'It is my unpleasant duty to inform you that you will be required to wind up your business here by the end of the month.'

Sally's jaw had dropped open. 'What are you talking about?'

'I think it's plain enough. I'm telling you you have to move out.'

'But you can't do that. It would destroy my business.' She swallowed. 'You have no right. You can't do that!'

'Oh, yes, I can.' His eyes bored through her as he lightly tossed the pot into the air once more.

Only, this time he did not catch it. He let it crash to the floor, scattering broken fragments like gunfire around their feet.

His eyes scanned Sally's pale face, then with a small sadistic smile he let his gaze drop pointedly to the wreckage on the floor.

'I can do it,' he told her, 'just as easily as that.'

CHAPTER TWO

SALLY'S heart had grown as still as a stone inside her. Bewildered, she stared at the broken pot on the floor. 'I had a buyer for that pot,' she told him in a dull tone.

But already Josh was reaching for his wallet, extracting a fifty-pound note and tossing it on to the counter beside her. 'That ought to cover it,' he said. 'I reckon that's more than you would have got for it, even in London.'

There he was with this London thing again! But Sally registered that only dimly. She was still half stunned by what he'd just told her.

She found her voice. 'What did you mean,' she demanded, 'when you said I have to wind up my business here and be out by the end of the month?'

'Precisely that. I think it's plain enough. These premises will no longer be available for rent.'

'But you can't mean it!' Her blood was churning as she gripped the edge of the counter, certain that if she let go she'd fall in a heap to the floor. 'I have a perfectly legal lease on this place...' Then she stopped in her tracks, her confusion suddenly illuminated by an icy glimmer of understanding.

Sally swallowed as she demanded, 'Is what you're trying to tell me that the lease on the shop is not to be renewed?'

'That's precisely what I'm telling you.' Hard black eyes looked back at her. 'Your current lease agreement runs out this month, and unfortunately I have to advise you that it is not to be renewed.'

'But that's ridiculous! That can't be! Your aunt Mimi told me that the lease would be renewed automatically. I spoke to her less than a fortnight ago. We were going to sign the papers next week!'

'There has been a change of plan.' With the toe of his shoe, Josh pushed the pieces of the shattered pot aside. 'There will be no signing of papers, next week or ever. Your lease on the shop is not to be renewed.'

'But your aunt Mimi said...' Sally could not believe what he was telling her. It couldn't be true. Surely she must be having a nightmare? 'She said it would be renewed... She said there'd be no problem.'

'Well, it would appear there is now.' Josh smiled a grim smile. 'You will be required to make alternative arrangements.'

'But how can I do that? At such short notice?' Sally stared at the pieces of the broken pot on the floor. Suddenly she knew exactly how that pot felt. 'I can't possibly find new premises in such a short time.'

'Then you'll have to close your business down.' He smiled with evil satisfaction. 'That would appear to be your only alternative.'

Sally felt a shiver go through her as she looked into his face. It would seem she'd been wrong about Josh all these years. He didn't just have a low opinion of her. It went much deeper than that. Quite clearly, he hated her.

She raised her eyes to his, the dull thud of her heart suddenly sounding like a death-knell in her ears. 'This is your doing, isn't it? You've persuaded your aunt. You're the one who's talked her into doing this!'

Josh did not deny it. He was clearly unrepentant. 'Fortunately, my aunt has always heeded my advice.'

'Then I shall just have to speak to her and persuade her not to this time.' As she defied him, Sally felt a sudden surge of optimism within her. She and the old lady had always got on well. There was hope, after all, that this calamity could be reversed.

But, instantly, Josh proceeded to douse her hope. 'I'm afraid that won't be possible. Aunt Mimi is out of the country. She's gone to visit her sister in Australia.'

'I don't believe you! When did she go to Australia?'

Josh glanced at his watch. 'This morning, just after breakfast. She should be somewhere over Asia by now.'

Sally stared at him in silence. He wasn't joking. In a shocked whisper she observed, 'You arranged this, too, didn't you? You arranged that she should be out of the country, so I couldn't talk her round.'

He did not deny that either. He simply looked back at her, unblinking. 'Aunt Mimi is no longer young. I wished her to avoid any unpleasantness. And besides,' he added with a quick, callous smile, 'she's been talking about visiting her sister for years. It seemed the perfect moment had arrived.'

Sally sagged against the counter. This really was a nightmare. Only unfortunately it was of the kind that happened for real.

She felt suddenly helpless. She raised her eyes. 'Why?'

'Now we come to the interesting bit.' The question seemed to please him. Josh paused and let his eyes travel over her unhurriedly. 'This is the bit I've been looking forward to telling you.'

She could see that in his eyes. They positively glowed with ruthless pleasure. She narrowed her own eyes against the pain they inflicted and fought a sudden surge of nausea. 'Tell me, then,' she said in a small, unsteady voice.

He did not answer immediately. Instead, taking his time, he continued to study her, with a slight curling around his lips, as though she were something unpleasant he'd found on his pillow.

Then he raised one dark eyebrow. 'I've found out about you,' he said.

Sally looked back at him in bafflement. 'Found out what about me?' she demanded.

Josh shook his head. 'That's right, deny it. It's really no more than I'd expected you'd do.'

'Deny what?' Sally blinked at him. 'I don't even know what you're talking about!'

'I think you do.'

'Then you're wrong, I don't! Tell me what I'm supposed to have done!'

Again Josh paused. Then he turned away impatiently. 'I think I've had enough of this for the moment. I'll come back and speak to both of you when your partner returns. I'd like what's his name—Clive—to hear first-hand the rest of what I have to say.'

'But he won't be back until tomorrow and I want to know now!' As he began to head for the door,

Sally lurched after him. Her legs felt like shredded paper beneath her. 'You can't go without telling me what's going on!'

'I'm afraid I can.' His hand was on the door-handle. 'I've told you all you need to know for now. In the meantime, until I come back tomorrow, why not make good use of your time?' He fixed her with a rapier look. 'You could, for example, start packing up your things.'

Then, leaving Sally fuming impotently in the doorway, he was climbing into the red Ferrari and, with a growl and a squeal of tyres, heading off down the road.

After Josh had gone, like an automaton, Sally shut up the shop, then headed on foot for the nearby Dovecote Flats, where she lived.

This can't be happening, she kept thinking, over and over. Any minute, I'm going to wake up and discover it was a bad dream.

But, deep down, she knew it wasn't a dream. Josh really did intend to put her out of business.

In her small first-floor flat she made a pot of tea and sank down at the kitchen table, feeling numb from head to toe. Perhaps I ought to phone Clive. The thought went through her head. Maybe I should tell him to come home straight away.

Clive, after all, as her partner in the business, had a right to know what was going on. And, besides, Josh had said that he wanted Clive present when he revealed the reason for what he was doing to them. The sooner Clive came back, the sooner they would know.

But, though she stared at the phone for a while, Sally didn't pick it up. This is between Josh and me, a voice kept telling her. It would serve no purpose and simply upset Clive if she were to phone and demand his urgent return.

After a couple of cups of tea Sally felt a little calmer and an idea had begun to take shape in her head. More and more, she was growing certain that Josh's motives were personal, somehow tied up with his deep dislike of her that she had never before suspected, and that each time she thought of it sent a chill through her blood.

And since it was a personal matter it ought to be dealt with personally. Face to face, between the two of them. There was really no reason for Clive to be present.

She stood up and paced the floor. If only she could face him now. If only she could have this whole thing out in the open, know what was really going on and be in a position to deal with it. She knew she wouldn't have a quiet moment until she did.

So what was she waiting for? The question flashed across her brain. Why didn't she go to him right now and tackle him?

Sally allowed the idea to settle for a moment. He'd be furious, of course, at her having the temerity to barge in on him at the mansion, uninvited. But what did she care? Sally squared her shoulders. Let him be furious. She had a right to know.

Half an hour later, showered and changed, her heart as tight as a fist in her chest, Sally was driving through the gentle summer twilight to Aunt Mimi's big old rambling house, where so many of her most vivid childhood memories had been born, to face Josh's wrath for better or worse.

The worst that could happen was that he would throw her out—but Sally refused to dwell on that thought. Instead, she focused on the best—the faint possibility that if, as she suspected, this decision of his was simply based on his irrational dislike of her, she might, just possibly, be able to change his mind.

Holding tightly to that hope, she turned in through the gates that opened on to the imposing tree-lined driveway that swept up to the front of the big, sprawling house.

Aunt Mimi's housekeeper opened the door.

'I've come to see Josh—Mr Kingsley,' Sally told her. 'I'm Sally Woodstock. Is he in?'

'Yes, he's in.'

Sally felt her heart thud, as, before the housekeeper had a chance to answer, Josh had appeared at the end of the hallway. Hands in trouser pockets, he approached her. 'But he was not aware that you and he had an appointment.'

'We don't.'

Sally was still standing on the doorstep, hating the way her heart had thudded at the sight of him—and wondering too if, while she had the chance, she ought to step boldly over the threshold.

But she refrained. If he wished, he could eject her from the hallway just as easily as from the front doorstep. The only difference was that the former would be marginally more embarrassing.

She said in a reasonable tone, 'I was hoping you might not be busy. That you might be able to spare me an hour of your time.'

'Were you, now? That was most optimistic. Why would I wish to spoil my evening by spending it with you?'

That hurt. More than it should have. Sally snatched a calming breath. 'I won't take up your whole evening. Just an hour or so, as I said.' She smiled a conciliatory smile. 'In fact, maybe less.'

'I'm still not tempted.' Josh remained standing facing her, feet planted in the centre of the Oriental rug. 'I can definitely think of pleasanter ways of spending an hour.'

And as he stood there looking down at her, dark eyes harsh and implacable, Sally was certain he was about to send her packing. But then something quite unexpected happened.

'Josh, I'm ready to leave now.' Through a doorway at the end of the hallway appeared a slender dark-haired figure whom Sally recognised instantly. It was Karin Stokes, a local potter. A girl Sally had known all her life.

No one would have guessed it from Karin's behaviour.

Approaching Josh, she slipped an arm through his and proceeded down the hall without even a glance in Sally's direction. And when Sally, slightly stunned, offered a tentative, 'Hi, Karin,' she simply looked right through her as though she weren't there.

Then she and Josh were sweeping past her and heading down the steps to the driveway where a small blue car, evidently Karin's, was parked.

Sally stood and watched frozenly as kisses were exchanged before Karin at last climbed into her car and drove off slowly down the driveway. And suddenly Sally's heart was clattering inside her, her insides squirming as though squeezed by red-hot pincers.

I'm simply mad at that snub, she told herself firmly. After all, I sold some of her work for her just recently! I don't give a damn about what's going on between her and Josh!

All the same, she averted her gaze as Josh waved Karin off—virtually until she had disappeared from sight!—and she was still calming her racing heart as Josh headed back towards her, hurrying up the stone steps to deliver her a none-too-friendly glance.

'Are you still here?' he demanded down his nose at her.

'Apparently so.' Sally met his gaze frostily. Then, forcing herself to remember what she'd come for, she softened her expression. 'An hour is all I ask.'

He did not answer her. He stepped past her into the hallway. And the housekeeper—who had remained hovering by the door all this time!—was just about to close the door behind him when he turned round suddenly.

'What are you waiting for? You'd better come in.'

With a sigh of relief Sally darted past the housekeeper. She was still a long way from achieving her objective, but at least she now had both feet inside the door!

Josh led her—or at least she followed him, running to catch up with him—across the hallway and through the open doorway of the room from which Karin only moments ago had appeared. And for an instant Sally forgot about everything else. Being inside this house again, this house she had known so well once, was bringing back an unstoppable flood of memories. The intensity of those memories clutched at her throat.

'Make yourself comfortable.'

Josh was waving her to one of the sofas. Then he cast her a sideways glance as he seated himself in a chair opposite. 'But then I scarcely need to observe such formalities with you. You know your way around this place as well as I do.'

'I did once, but it's a long time since I've been here.' Sally seated herself on the edge of the sofa. It must be all of seven years, she calculated quickly, but in a funny way it felt like yesterday.

'I don't think it's changed much.'

'It's changed hardly at all.'

Sally glanced round at the elegant, tastefully furnished room, with its antique furniture and paintings on the walls, and observed that it was still more or less as it had been all those years ago when she had known it so well.

In those days, her mother had cooked for Aunt Mimi, Josh's much-loved widowed aunt, and Sally, from time to time, had had the privilege of accompanying her. To her this house had seemed a magical place. She could still feel its magic even now.

'Aunt Mimi was always a bit of a traditionalist. She likes things to stay the way they are.'

As he spoke, Josh reached towards the low mahogany coffee-table, picked up the half-full brandy glass that lay there, took a quick mouthful and set it down again. And that was when Sally suddenly noticed what were evidently the remains of an informal little supper—plates and cutlery, coffee-cups and wine glasses—piled on a tray at one corner of the table.

And there were two of everything, she noted with a jolt—rather like the jolt she had experienced earlier at the sight of Josh and Karin kissing. The two of them had obviously just shared a cosy little supper.

So, why should I care? Sally told herself firmly, quickly dousing the unwelcome sensation that flooded through her.

The housekeeper had appeared and was clearing away the tray. As she left the room, Josh sat back in his armchair and narrowed his treacle-black eyes at Sally.

'Why don't you get started? Several minutes of that hour you asked for have already passed. I'm sure you don't want to waste any more of it.'

Ah, yes. Once more Sally dragged her thoughts back to what she was here for. And, remembering, she looked back at him with a pleasing snap of antipathy.

'I see you're timing me,' she said.

By way of a response Josh glanced at his watch. 'You have less than fifty-five minutes left.'

Sally straightened in her seat. She'd better get on with it. Since it seemed he really did plan on showing her the door the very instant her hour was up, there was no point in sitting here wasting it in futile bickering!

Looking him in the eye, she put to him, 'I want to know why you want me out of the shop.'

'I thought I told you we'd discuss that to-morrow?' Josh reached again for the brandy glass and took another mouthful. 'In the company of your boyfriend.'

'I know. But I'd like to discuss it now. I don't think it's necessary for Clive to be present.'

One dark eyebrow lifted in a mockery of disapproval. 'Is Clive aware of this somewhat cavalier attitude you have regarding his involvement in company business?'

Yes, that was what it sounded like. Sally bit her lip and frowned at him. 'I don't have a cavalier attitude, as you call it. I don't keep things from Clive.' And neither she did. 'It just seems to me that this matter's rather different. It's clearly me, not Clive, you have some beef with.'

Josh smiled at that. 'You could be right.' He leaned his dark head against the cushions. His hair shone like black silk against the bright tapestry. 'But whoever my beef, as you call it, is with, as your partner in the business, Clive is as affected as much as you are. Which was why I stipulated that he be present.'

He looked so at ease, so utterly in control, as he leaned back against the tapestry cushions, his brandy glass held lightly in one sun-bronzed hand. And there was she, perched on the edge of the sofa, as though she were still that awestruck and vulnerable child of all those years ago.

But she had no reason to feel that way. Deliberately, Sally sat back a bit and forced herself to relax against the cushions.

'Why are you so worried about Clive?' she demanded, and instantly felt better for being on the offensive. 'It's not like you to show such concern for others.'

'Oh, don't worry, this isn't concern you're seeing.' Josh smiled to show how little her dig had bothered him. 'I simply prefer to have both partners present in order to save myself the trouble of repeating myself.'

'That won't be necessary. I'm perfectly capable of relaying whatever you tell me to Clive. There would be no need for you to repeat yourself.'

'And are you also capable of answering on Clive's behalf? Don't you think he'd prefer to do that for himself?'

'Yes, I think I can answer on Clive's behalf.' Sally regarded him with impatience. This was all so unnecessary. In other circumstances, *of course* she would want Clive present, but Josh knew as well as she did that this was between him and her. There was no reason in the world for Clive to be present.

She added for good measure, 'We have a very close partnership. We're each well acquainted with the views of the other. We answer for one another all the time.'

'How very cosy. Sounds like the ideal relationship.' Josh smiled a scathing smile. 'My congratulations.'

That was stretching it a bit. Ideal relationship. What she and Clive had was not exactly that. But she *was* lucky to have him, and the rest was none of Josh's business. She nodded in agreement. 'Yes, I am lucky,' she said.

'Where was it you met him?' Surveying her with interest, Josh crossed one leg at the ankle over the opposite knee. He was wearing shiny brown boots a shade or two darker than his trousers that were suddenly stretched more tautly over his strong, muscular thighs. 'Wasn't it while you were at art college in London?'

'Yes, it was.' Surprised at herself, Sally detached her eyes hurriedly from his thighs. What on earth were they doing there in the first place? she chided herself. The days when she'd responded to Josh's physical allure was surely well and truly behind her? Though that allure continued to be considerable, she consented.

'So, you've known him for some time?'

'It would appear so.'

'Five or six years.'

'You can add up, I see.'

Josh nodded and held her eyes. 'Oh, yes, I can add up. I have no trouble at all in putting two and two together.' He smiled a mysterious smile, making Sally wonder what he'd meant by that, then he continued, 'But returning to the subject of Clive...'

As he spoke, he swirled the brandy round in his glass. In the light from the table lamp it flashed and danced. 'One must get to know someone pretty well in the course of five or six years.'

'I suppose one does.'

With an eloquent flick of her eyes Sally reminded him that he and she had known each other a great deal longer, and that she, as a result, certainly knew *him* pretty well. And, what was more, did not much like what she knew.

'Quite so.' Josh smiled. He knew precisely what she was saying. The dark eyes held hers as he took another mouthful of brandy. 'So, as I was saying,' he continued, 'you must know Clive pretty well by now?'

'Pretty well, yes.' Though she might have added that, though they had been acquainted with one another for six years, during their college years they had not been particularly close and then there had been two whole years when they'd lost contact altogether. But why should she go into such details with Josh? Not even remotely did such details concern him.

'So when's the wedding going to be?'

Sally blinked at the question. 'Who said anything about a wedding?'

'A natural assumption.' Josh drained his brandy glass, then reached out and laid it on the table. 'When two people are so close and in business together, marriage would seem a natural development.'

That was more or less precisely what Clive had said. And perhaps it was true. Perhaps it would happen. But that, like all the rest, was none of Josh's business.

Sally tilted her chin at him. 'That's a surprise coming from you. I thought you didn't believe in marriage?'

He seemed to consider her statement. 'And what made you think that?'

'I seem to remember you saying it, more or less. Marriage and settling down, you said, weren't for you.' She paused before adding with more than a hint of disapproval, 'So many women and so little time. I seem to remember you telling me that was your philosophy.'

'Did I say that?' Josh smiled, considering. 'I suppose I might have. After all, it's true. When there are so many dishes to enjoy, why should one put oneself on a diet?'

Sally laughed a scathing laugh. 'So many dishes to enjoy. That really is how you think of women, isn't it?'

Yet, all the same, in spite of her disapproval, she was aware of a sneaking, shameful feeling of satisfaction as an image of Karin suddenly popped into her head. Karin would last no longer than any of the others. She disliked how satisfied that made her feel.

To redeem herself, she added, her tone suitably cutting, 'I've always disapproved of your attitude to women. You used to change girlfriends more regularly than most boys change their socks.'

'Did I really? Frankly, I wasn't counting.'

'No, I suppose you weren't. They weren't important to you. All they were were fleeting conquests.'

'How well you sum it up.' Josh shook his head wryly. 'You know, I can't even remember who most of them were.'

Of course he couldn't. Who could possibly remember? Even Sally could only recall a few faces!

'No doubt,' she put to him, 'your philosophy remains unchanged?'

'So many women and so little time?' He smiled. 'Can you suggest a better one?'

He was shameless and irresponsible. Sally looked into his face, at the dark eyes that looked back at her, bright with amusement. It made no difference that he had it so easy, that women fell at his feet. He ought to be capable of behaving better.

She thought of Karin again and of her own less than sisterly thoughts a moment ago and proceeded to redeem herself further as she accused him, 'Does Karin know about your philosophy?'

'Karin?'

'Yes. Karin.' Her eyebrows rose as he stared back, puzzled. 'Don't tell me you've forgotten about her already?' This was fast work, even for him! she was thinking. 'You only kissed her goodbye a couple of minutes ago.'

'Ah... *That* Karin!'

'How many are there?'

'How many Karins? I suspect a few. After all, it's a fairly common name.' Then Josh paused and smiled across at her. 'Perhaps you ought to warn her of the terrible danger she's in.'

There was a look in his eyes, amused and teasing, that caught Sally totally unawares. It was a look she'd seen a thousand times, just like all his other looks. I know him so well, she thought with a sudden rush of emotion. I know him, but he doesn't know me.

She pushed these feelings from her and forced her thoughts back to the present.

'I wouldn't dream of interfering in your personal life,' she told him. 'And besides,' she added, straightening, 'that's not why I came... in order to talk about your conquests. What I want is for you to tell me why you want to close my business. I think you owe it to me to be frank.'

'I'll be frank enough in due course.' He was no longer smiling, for which Sally found herself feeling deeply grateful. It was his smiles, more than anything, that tended to unsteady her. His scowls were much, much easier to cope with.

'I've already told you,' he was continuing, 'I'll reveal my reasons when I have your partner before me as well as yourself.'

'But that's not necessary!'

'Nevertheless, it's what I've decided.'

Josh had folded his arms like a barrier against her. The expression in his eyes was suddenly touched with ice. He looked as though nothing could move him as Sally protested, 'Why must you prolong the agony? I have a right to know, with or without Clive! And, what's more, you have a duty to tell me!'

'You dare to talk about rights? What do you care about rights?' All at once Josh seemed to explode with anger. Every muscle in his body seemed to tense and quiver. 'I would advise you not to have the temerity to talk to me about rights—nor to try to tell me where my duty lies!'

Sally was taken aback by the sudden change in him. She had seen him angry before, but never like this. But she was angry, too, and she had every right to be. Here he was, calmly threatening to ruin her, and he didn't even have the decency to tell her why he was doing it!

'And why shouldn't I tell you?' she shot back at him. 'You seem to need telling! You can't just treat people the way you're treating me and walk away without an explanation!'

'I'm not walking away. You'll have your explanation.' His tone was tempered steel, controlled but dangerous. 'You'll have your explanation when I'm ready to give it.'

'Well, that's not good enough! I want it now! In fact, I demand it now, and I won't leave until I get it!'

'Oh, won't you?' A flash of harsh humour touched his eyes. 'I'm afraid you're wrong about that. You're leaving right this minute!'

He had risen to his feet and was standing over her. 'Right now,' he repeated. 'And it will be my pleasure to escort you.'

Sally glared at him, defiant. 'I haven't had my hour yet. You said you would give me an hour of your time!'

'In that case, I must apologise.' Every syllable clashed like cymbals. 'I must have forgotten how distasteful an hour with you can be. As it is, the brief time we've had has been more than enough. And now...' he gestured towards the door '...I'd be grateful if you'd leave.'

Still Sally did not budge. She glared at him mutinously. 'I'll bet Aunt Mimi doesn't know what you're up to. She would never stand for behaviour like this.' Then she frowned. 'What have you said to her? What lies have you told her to make her turn against me like this?'

'Only the truth. That was quite adequate. No lies were called for.'

As he spoke, in one movement he whisked her from the sofa. Sally gasped. She had never moved so fast in her life! Then, before she could recover, he was propelling her out into the hall, then reaching in front of her and pulling open the front door.

'I'll tell you this much before you go.' For a moment he held her where she stood. 'Since you're so desperate to know my reasons . . . here they are. I'm going to evict you because you're a disgusting little thief.' He gave her a shake. 'But your thieving days are over. And this time you're going to pay dearly for your crimes.'

He released her abruptly. 'I think I need say no more.' Then, his hand on the door, he invited her, 'Now leave. Immediately. Unless you want me to throw you out.'

Sally barely heard that last part. Already she was running towards her van, sick to her soul, her stomach churning inside her. But she heard the thunder of the front door as it slammed violently behind her.

CHAPTER THREE

OH, WHAT shame!

Sally died a thousand deaths that night as she relived those last few minutes of her encounter with Josh. It had all been so much like that other time, all those years ago, only more violent, more direct, more crushing to her soul. Last time he had merely hinted at what he'd said out loud tonight.

He believed she was a thief and that was why he despised her. That was why he wanted her out of his aunt Mimi's shop.

But she was no thief. She never had been. Yet, somehow, she had never managed to tell him the truth.

The whole catastrophe had happened when she was eleven years old, before she had conquered her feelings for Josh. For, though she hated to admit it now—she even denied it to herself sometimes!—there had been a time when, like every other female, she had sighed for Josh and fallen under his spell.

Of course she had! How could she have done otherwise? From the first time she had set eyes on him at the innocent age of six he had seemed to her the most beautiful and exciting creature in the world.

'This is my nephew,' she remembered Aunt Mimi telling her, that day when she'd gone to the big house with her mother. It had been during the school holidays and her mother had been reluctant

47

to leave her alone at home while she was out working. And, anyway, Aunt Mimi—or Mrs Moore, as her mother called her—had insisted that her cook's daughter was always welcome.

'Joshua, look after Sally. Have a game of table tennis or something,' Aunt Mimi had instructed, after she'd made the introductions. Then she'd left them. 'Try to have a nice time together.'

As it turned out, Sally had a very nice time, but Josh, she suspected, would gladly have done without the encounter. Thirteen-year-old boys, after all, didn't exactly revel in the company of little girls seven years their junior!

But it had to be said of Josh that he couldn't have been kinder to her.

'Do you often come here?' he'd asked her politely, as he'd led her to the ping-pong table out on the patio.

'Only during the holidays when my mother doesn't want to leave me.' Then she'd added brightly, 'But I like it here.'

'Me, too.' At least on that point they'd agreed! 'Really, I live in London, but quite often I come here when my parents are off abroad.'

Sally had regarded him curiously. 'Why don't they take you with them?' She couldn't imagine her own parents going off and leaving her!

'Because I don't want to go with them.' As he'd answered swiftly and firmly, dispersing instantly the flicker of regret that had touched his eyes, Sally had caught her first glimpse of the independence of spirit that was to become such a central part of his character. She'd sensed the strength that flowed from him and she'd felt it draw her.

'So, where do you live? Do you live in the village?' he'd asked her as they prepared to play their first game.

'We live in one of the cottages down by the post office. Ours,' she'd added proudly, 'is the one with the red front door.'

Josh had smiled. 'I have a friend who used to live in one of those cottages, though I don't think his had a red front door.' Then he'd taken a coin from his pocket. 'Shall we toss for ends?'

They'd played a couple of games and Josh had let her win both of them. How else could she have won? She was utterly hopeless! And though she'd sensed he was relieved when, soon afterwards, they'd parted, she'd decided that Josh was a really nice boy. That had been the start of her crush.

It had grown as, in the beginning, he'd continued to be nice to her. Each time they met he'd ask how she was doing and make her smile with a joke or some story. There had even been a couple more games of table tennis! But he never lingered in her company and she was never a part of his group. She was always on the sidelines, watching.

Not that Sally minded. When Josh's friends came round—a bunch of noisy, rumbustious thirteen-year-olds—she would sit quietly reading a book, preferably one of Aunt Mimi's art books, and just enjoy from a distance their energetic goings-on. Though most of all, of course, it was watching Josh that she enjoyed.

But things started to change when the girlfriends began appearing.

Sometimes they came singly, sometimes there'd be groups of them, all giggling at nothing, following Josh around like puppies and fluttering their silly mascaraed eyelashes at him. And he, of course, lapped up their admiration and barely seemed to notice Sally any more. And that was when she began to feel like an outsider.

She'd sit quietly in a corner, pretending to colour in her drawing book, and all the while she'd be watching beneath her lashes as Josh stole the heart of his latest teenage admirer. For he stole the hearts of all of them. Sally knew that. She recognised that look in their eyes all too well.

For the most part, these girls ignored her. To them she was just a kid. But there was one, the blue-eyed Lucinda—now long gone from the village—who seemed to have taken an irrational dislike to Sally and always made a point of looking daggers at her.

And then one day Lucinda had spoken to her.

'So who's the mouse in the corner?' she'd said.

Sally remembered very clearly those first endearing words. Josh was out of the room at the time and Lucinda had come over to the window, where Sally was seated with her sketchpad and pencils.

Pausing in her drawing, she'd glanced up into the other girl's china-blue eyes. 'I'm not a mouse,' she'd said evenly. 'I'm Sally.'

'Sally?' Lucinda had sneered. 'What a common name. You're one of the village girls, aren't you? Your mother's a servant.'

Sally had felt herself bridle. Who did Lucinda think she was? 'Yes, I live in the village,' she'd answered, her sea-green eyes sparking. 'But my mother's not a servant. She's a *cordon bleu* cook.

Aunt Mimi says she's the best cook in the whole of England.'

'Aunt Mimi? Mrs Moore isn't *your* aunt Mimi!' Lucinda had pounced on her, outraged by this familiarity. 'Does she know you call her that?'

'Of course she knows. I've always called her Aunt Mimi.'

'Well, I think you have a nerve! A girl like you, who doesn't even belong here!' The china-blue eyes had swept over her dismissively. 'But I suppose, out of politeness, she's just trying to be kind.'

That had hurt, unexpectedly and deeply. Sally had always believed that Aunt Mimi was fond of her and that that was why she had always been so kind to her.

Just for a moment she'd been unable to answer. And it was at that very moment that Josh had reappeared.

Lucinda had turned to beam at him. 'I was just chatting to Sally. She was showing me some of her lovely drawings.'

'Yes, Sally's quite an artist.' Josh had come to stand beside them. 'I'm always telling her she's got a special talent.' Josh had bent to look at her half-finished drawing. 'I wish I had a talent like that.'

Sally remembered sitting there, feeling patronised and deeply uncomfortable, and wondering suddenly whether, if what Lucinda had said was true—that Aunt Mimi only put up with her out of politeness—perhaps the same was true also of Josh?

Perhaps, out of politeness, he had only ever *pretended* to like her. The thought had sent a cold chill round her heart.

As she had sat there in growing misery, she'd heard Lucinda giggle, 'You have other talents, Josh.' And she gave his cheek a playful tweak. 'And I'll vouch for that any time you like!'

In response, to Sally's total mortification, Josh had bent down and planted a quick kiss on Lucinda's lips. 'You're pretty talented yourself,' he'd answered.

Then the two of them had departed, arms wrapped round one another, leaving Sally feeling crushed and utterly humiliated. For the first time in all the long years she'd been going to Aunt Mimi's she'd suddenly felt she had no right to be there, that she was only there on sufferance, an unwelcome pariah. Heartbroken, she'd made a vow that she'd never come back.

Of course, the vow got broken, though perhaps, she had often thought, it might have been better if it hadn't. If it hadn't, that final catastrophe would never have happened.

It was partly Aunt Mimi's art books that had lured Sally back. For years now she'd been going through them, poring over their wondrous pages, drinking in the beauty she found there. Only she hadn't seen them all yet. Aunt Mimi had kept aside some of the more valuable volumes till she was older. It was just after her eleventh birthday that her mother had relayed the message that she would now be permitted to see the 'special' books. How could she resist such an offer when she'd been waiting for it for years?

And so, six months after that brush with Lucinda, Sally found herself once more a guest in the Moore mansion. And who also should be there but Josh and Lucinda?

'Oh, it's so gorgeous! I really love it!'

Suddenly Lucinda, with Josh at her heels, had burst into the drawing-room where Sally was sitting. She'd rushed up to the gilt-framed mirror and let out another exclamation. 'Oh, Josh, it's so exquisite! I couldn't possibly!'

'Of course, you can. In fact, I insist.' Josh had come to stand behind Lucinda at the mirror. Then he'd reached out to touch the garnet necklace at her throat. 'It looks fabulous on you. I knew it would.'

And it did look fabulous, Sally had to agree, as she glanced up, heart suddenly racing, from her book on Monet. Though it wasn't the sight of the necklace that had made her heart race. It was the sudden, unexpected sight of Josh.

And suddenly she knew that it wasn't just the art books that had lured her back to Aunt Mimi's mansion. In her heart she had desperately wanted to see Josh again.

He hadn't noticed her at first, but now he spied her. 'What do you think?' He was propelling Lucinda towards her. 'You're the artist. Is this a work of art, or what?'

He was mocking her, of course. The dark eyes flashed with amusement. Sally suddenly felt as sensitive as a raw, exposed nerve-end.

'You mean the necklace?' she'd said, blinking and smoothing back her hair. 'Yes, the necklace is very pretty.'

Somehow it had come out sounding mean and covetous. The necklace was exquisite, and so was its wearer. She saw one black eyebrow lift. Josh had noted her reaction.

'I'm wearing it to the dinner tonight,' Lucinda told her, flashing a smile at Josh. 'We're having a special celebration for my eighteenth birthday.'

'Congratulations.' Again it came out sounding grudging. Suddenly all Sally could think of was that that exquisite garnet necklace must be a birthday gift from Josh.

Such a very special gift. An expression of love, surely? In that moment, from the very bottom of her heart, fiercely, bitterly, Sally envied Lucinda.

It was to hide those feelings that she dropped her eyes back to her book. She knew it was rude, that it simply made her look worse. But it was the only way her eleven-year-old heart could handle the emotions that were pouring through her.

'We'll leave you to your books.'

She heard them move away, and she hated the cold note she could detect in Josh's voice. Then, in a room across the hall, a phone began to ring. 'That'll be for me,' she heard Josh say. 'I won't be a minute.'

Sally didn't look up as she heard footsteps head out to the hall. She wasn't sure if Lucinda had left the room, too. For a minute or two she remained staring at her book, the pictures a blur, her heart in turmoil, not knowing why she felt the way she did, only wishing she had never come back to the mansion.

Then something made her glance up. It was as though she felt eyes on her. And, sure enough, there was Lucinda standing in the doorway, the china-blue eyes fixed on her face. Then, with an odd little smile, and touching the necklace at her throat, she disappeared out into the hall.

Sally waited five minutes, then gathered up her books and replaced them carefully on the bookshelves. Home, she was thinking. Suddenly she had to escape.

She stepped out into the hall. Aunt Mimi was out, so she was spared having to explain her early departure. But, as she turned and started to head towards the front door, something on the marble-topped side-table caught her eye.

Sally stopped in her tracks. It was the garnet necklace. Her heart flipped over as she bent to look down at it. What on earth was it doing here?

It would have been wiser if she'd kept going and just pretended she'd never seen it. But she didn't. Instead, she approached the little table and picked it up.

I'd better find Lucinda, she was thinking. She can't leave the necklace here. Someone could take it.

But, as she held it in her hand, this beautiful object, this gift that Josh had chosen for Lucinda's birthday, she was suddenly filled with an overwhelming desire to see what it would look like round her own neck.

Not thinking what she was doing or how it might look, she crossed to the nearby cloakroom and pushed open the door. Then, standing before the mirror, she slipped the necklace round her neck and fastened the clasp with trembling fingers.

'So you like it, do you?'

Sally spun round, her cheeks flaming, to find Lucinda standing in the doorway, watching her.

The china-blue eyes were filled with malice. 'Funny, I thought something like this might happen.'

It was sheer panic and confusion, nothing more sinister, that caused Sally to react the way she did. She clutched her hand to her throat, hiding the necklace beneath her T-shirt. 'I—I thought you were in the other drawing-room,' she stuttered, making the situation worse.

'Well, I'm not, am I? And I reckon it's just as well. It looks as though I've caught you red-handed.'

Sally's jaw dropped open. 'Red-handed?' she mouthed.

And then Josh appeared. 'What's going on here?' he demanded. He was standing behind Lucinda, one hand on her shoulder.

'It's her!' There were tears of outrage in Lucinda's voice as she pointed an accusing finger at Sally. 'She's taken the necklace. Look! She's trying to hide it! She's trying to hide it under her T-shirt!'

There was a silence, like the moment before an execution, as Josh stood there, dark eyes narrowed, watching Sally for a moment. Then he said in a quiet voice that made her skin shiver, 'Is this true, Sally? Have you taken the necklace?'

Sally could not speak. She shook her head mutely. It's not what it looks like, she wanted to say. But that look in Josh's eyes had torn her tongue out.

Then Lucinda suddenly shrieked, 'Liar! You have got it!' And she leapt forward, grabbing the front of Sally's T-shirt, to reveal, for all the world to see, the garnet necklace.

Sally would never forget Josh's reaction. The muscles around his jawline seemed to harden and a look that would send nightmares to haunt her for years suddenly smouldered at the back of his eyes.

He said, 'Take it off.' Then he held out his hand. 'And hand it over to me immediately.'

'I left it on the hall table. I suppose, really, it was my fault.' The china-blue eyes glinted venomously at Sally. 'But then I didn't know there were thieves in the house.'

'None of us knew.' Josh's tone was like granite as Sally slipped off the necklace and dropped it into his hand. He flayed her with a look. 'How could you do it? After all Aunt Mimi's done for you, how could you steal her necklace?'

'I didn't know it was Aunt Mimi's!' It was the wrong thing to say, of course, but Sally wasn't thinking very straight.

As Lucinda elaborated, 'She lent it to me to wear to the dinner tonight,' suddenly, illogically, the principal thought in Sally's head was that the necklace was not a present from Josh, after all. It was not the gift of love she had imagined. At that moment that should not have mattered, but somehow it did.

'I won't tell Aunt Mimi. That would only hurt her too much.' Through the fog in her head she was aware of Josh speaking. 'But I forbid you to set foot in this house ever again. Do you understand me? From now on you'll stay away.'

'Yes, I understand, but——'

'But nothing,' Josh cut in before she could continue, and the look in his eyes caused her soul to shiver. She felt something within her retreat as he added in a steely tone, 'If I ever hear you've set foot in this house again, you'll be sorry, that I can promise you.'

'I don't want to set foot in here again, so you don't have to threaten me!' She couldn't believe that Josh would speak to her like this. She'd done nothing to deserve it! She hadn't stolen the necklace! How could he believe she had?

But her protestations remained unspoken, locked inside her. It was as though he'd crushed her will to give them voice.

He stood aside. 'You may go now. And don't forget what I've told you. Don't ever come back.'

Sally had rushed past him, ashen-faced, her heart in splinters. 'Don't worry, I won't!' And then, in tears, she fled home.

It was in fact six years before she set foot in the mansion again. Six years, during which, after much weeping and misery, she'd finally managed to banish Josh from her heart and turn her old admiration for him into dislike. She was seventeen years old and at the request of her mother, who was laid up in bed with a bad dose of the flu, had stopped off to drop in a Christmas card to Aunt Mimi.

But Aunt Mimi had been in the garden and, as soon as she'd seen Sally, she'd insisted that she come indoors for a sherry.

'I won't take no for answer,' she'd told the reluctant Sally, leading her across the hall and into the drawing-room—where, to Sally's mute horror, Josh was sitting.

At the sight of him she'd almost bolted. The only reason she didn't was because her feet were suddenly glued to the floor. She'd seen him fleetingly, once, since that débâcle about the necklace, but this was the first time for six years that she'd looked directly into his face. And, though such a thing wasn't possible, he was even more handsome than before.

He was dressed in casual trousers and a blue cashmere sweater, his dark hair a little long, a little wild-looking, as usual, his skin tanned, every inch of him radiating vitality. His features had lost the boyish softness of adolescence. They were more sharply defined now, and it was a look that suited him. But his eyes were unchanged. They had always been bold eyes. As dangerous and as black and as inviting as sin.

Neither had he lost any of his old *savoir-faire*. He proceeded to handle the situation with perfect ease, acting as though he was pleased to see her. Aunt Mimi didn't suspect a thing.

'How grown-up you've become.' The black eyes had travelled over her in a way they never had before. 'I scarcely recognised you any more.'

'Oh, she's quite the little lady. And she'll be off to London soon.' Aunt Mimi had smiled warmly as she handed her a small sherry. 'Next year she's going off to art school.'

'Now that doesn't surprise me. I always said she had talent.' Josh had cast an almost benevolent gaze on Sally. 'I'm very pleased to hear it,' he'd told her. 'It would be a shame to waste such talent.'

Sally had stared into her sherry, wishing she could drown in it, resisting the nervous urge to reach up and smooth her hair. Every time she looked at Josh, as vivid as yesterday, she remembered that soul-destroying scene in the cloakroom, the worthless way he had made her feel and all the cruel things he'd said.

And behind the smile he still believed she was a thief. The thought made her shudder. But it also made her angry. How could he believe such a vile thing?

'Joshua's down in London, as you probably know. At least, part of the time.' Aunt Mimi had smiled a fond smile. 'That is, when he's not jetting about all over the world.'

Sally had heard about Josh's successes, about his various flourishing businesses. Still only twenty-five, he was something of a tycoon.

She said, clutching at her anger, banishing her shame, as she looked at him, 'You seem to have become such an important person these days that I'm surprised you have time to visit our little village.'

'I make time to visit it—or rather to visit Aunt Mimi. That's the least I can do. Aunt Mimi has always been good to me.'

It was a subtle rebuke and also a reminder that he had not forgotten that business with the necklace—and that he still despised her for having betrayed Aunt Mimi, who, after all, had been good to her, too.

Sally had glanced down into her lap, smoothing her skirt, making herself look even more guilty. She could not hold his gaze, knowing what he believed, even though it was a million miles from the truth. She could never have betrayed Aunt Mimi. The very idea was shameful.

'Maybe you'll be able to see each other when Sally goes up to London.' Aunt Mimi had no idea what was going on. She turned to Sally. 'I'm sure Joshua would help you if you needed help with anything. And it would be good for you to know you had a big brother on hand.'

At that, quite spontaneously, Sally and Josh had looked at one another and an amused, knowing smile had passed between them. Josh, a big brother? He'd never be that to her! But, though they'd both thought the same thing, it had been for entirely different reasons.

On Sally's part, even when she was little, she'd never thought of Josh as a big brother. He'd been too special, too magical, to fall into such a mundane category. And now the idea was alien simply because she disliked him.

Josh, for his part, had probably never considered that they had any kind of relationship at all! Sally suspected that for most of the time she'd simply been invisible to him!

And, needless to say, Sally did not see Josh in London. Throughout her entire three years at art school, happily, their paths didn't cross once. And since then till the moment when he'd surprised her at the postbox she'd set eyes on him only a couple of times.

One of those times had been fleeting and he hadn't even seen her. She'd been driving past the mansion and seen him walking in the driveway. The other had been eighteen months ago and it had not been pleasant.

She'd been with Clive at the time. They'd been emerging from a local café and had almost walked straight into Josh. She remembered how, when she'd introduced them, he'd looked at Clive as though he were garbage, then had turned to fix her with that piercing black gaze of his.

'I hear you've taken over the shop.' His disapproval was tangible. Then he'd looked her up and down. 'We'll see,' he'd said ominously. Then, leaving them both bewildered, he'd turned and walked away.

And that was the sad history of Josh and Sally. Only now it had taken a turn for the worse. Now, suddenly, things had become more overt and vicious. Now, suddenly, he was out for her blood.

Back home, after her ignominious departure from the mansion, Sally lay on the sofa and stared at the ceiling, wondering what had sparked things off. His anger against her had lain dormant for years. What had triggered it into action now?

Something must have. It surely wasn't possible that he would just turn against her out of the blue like this, on the strength of one supposed crime that had taken place years ago? That just didn't feel right. But what else could it be?

As she pondered, the phone on the table beside the sofa rang. With a sigh, Sally reached out and lifted the receiver to her ear.

'Hello?' she said.

'Sally, it's Clive. How are you doing?'

'Clive? It's great to hear you!' Sally sat up with a relieved smile. She hadn't realised how desperately she was in need of a friendly voice. Then she frowned. 'If you really want to know, I'm not too terrific.'

'Why, love? What's the matter?' Clive was instantly concerned. 'Has something happened? Are you ill?'

'No, I'm not ill. But yes, something has happened.' Sally paused, dubious about spilling out the whole mess over the phone. 'Look, I'll tell you all about it when you get back tomorrow.' Then she added, 'But don't worry. I'm sure it's something we can sort out.'

'I'm worried already.' Clive's tone was serious. 'Come on, love, tell me what's going on.'

Sally felt instantly guilty. What a mess she'd got them into! And now, to make things worse, she'd got Clive worried.

'It's Aunt Mimi's nephew...Josh. Remember him? He's been round at the shop, making trouble...'

'What kind of trouble? Has he harmed you?'

'No, of course not.' The response was automatic. Josh was dangerous, but not in the way Clive was meaning. She hurried on, 'He's been making threats about the business——' Then she broke off. 'Look, let's not talk about it over the phone. I'll tell you everything when I see you. What time will you be back?'

There was a pause.

'Clive?'

Then he spoke, sounding anxious. 'I'll be back around lunchtime. You take care now. I'll see you soon. Goodnight, Sally. Sweet dreams.'

Fat chance, thought Sally, as she climbed between the sheets that night, though it was comforting to know that Clive would be back soon. At least there'd be somebody to give her a bit of support.

But that was all he'd be able to give her. Sally stared into the darkness. It was an ungenerous thought, but Clive was no match for Josh. And besides, she was still convinced of the fact that this battle was between herself and Josh.

She sighed and closed her eyes. She mustn't sell Clive short. She couldn't have managed without him over the past eighteen months. He might have put little in terms of cash into the business, but when it came to enthusiasm and effort his contribution had been boundless.

That made her feel guilty again. Now, thanks to her, Clive stood to lose all he'd worked so hard for. And that wasn't fair. In fact, it was outrageous. She simply couldn't allow it to happen!

And that was when she decided. Suddenly it came to her. If all her current problems sprang from that episode with the necklace, it was high time she dealt with that and let Josh know the truth. She hadn't done it before for a dozen different reasons—she'd told herself it didn't matter, that he wouldn't believe her. But now it *did* matter and, somehow, she must *make* him believe her.

She made herself a promise. First thing tomorrow morning she'd drive round to the mansion and tell Josh everything—and, hopefully, have the whole mess sorted out before Clive got back at lunchtime.

On that optimistic thought she drifted off to sleep.

Less than seven hours later she was awakened by the phone.

'Be round at my place within the hour.' It was Josh. 'And I mean within the hour.'

Sally blinked herself awake. 'I was planning to come round anyway.'

But she needn't have bothered answering. The phone had gone dead.

CHAPTER FOUR

'Do YOU enjoy dragging people out of their beds and then keeping them hanging around?'

Sally bunched her fists that were stuffed into her jeans pockets as she stood in the middle of his office at the mansion and glared daggers into Josh's sweater-clad back. 'I didn't even take time to have any breakfast!'

'In that case, you must be hungry.' He turned slowly to face her, switching off the computer monitor whose screen he'd been standing studying. 'I'll ask Mrs Lowe, the housekeeper, to put something together for you. What would you like?' The black eyes surveyed her. 'Cereal? Bacon and eggs? A cup of coffee?'

Damn his coolness! Sally glared back at him, tempted to tell him what to do with his offer. After rushing to be here within the hour, as commanded, she'd just spent thirty minutes twiddling her thumbs in the drawing-room and was in no mood for this display of false magnanimity.

But he was right, she was hungry, so she said instead, in a clipped tone, 'A cup of coffee and a slice of toast would be rather welcome.' Then she narrowed her sea-green eyes at him. 'But you haven't answered my question. Why did you demand to see me with such urgency when, quite clearly, the situation isn't even remotely urgent?'

'Perhaps, as you said, I enjoy dragging people out of bed, then keeping them hanging around for a while.' He had seated himself on the edge of the desk and was smiling that arrogantly amused smile that so maddened her. He lifted one eyebrow, his lips curling at the corners. 'And it was worth it. I've never seen you look so angry.'

'There's a lot you haven't seen!'

'Sounds promising.' His smile broadened. 'And you really do look quite stunning when you're mad.'

That old cliché! Sally tossed her head dismissively. Yet she was aware that her flushed cheeks had become even redder and that she'd very nearly succumbed to that old reflex action of reaching up quickly to touch her hair. The way he'd looked at her just then with those sinful black eyes of his had given her goosebumps from her scalp to her toes.

What's wrong with you? she chided herself, folding her arms across her chest. You're acting as though you were eleven years old again!

'So, why are you so mad, anyway? Is half an hour of your time so precious?' He cocked his head at her. 'Is it really worth getting so upset about?'

'I'm not upset. I'm just annoyed, and justifiably! Anyone would be annoyed at being treated so arrogantly. Summoned by a phone call at seven-thirty in the morning, then left hanging around waiting until you feel like seeing me!' She glared at him. 'You know, you've got a nerve!'

As he simply smiled back at her, unrepentant, it occurred to Sally that his hair was a trifle more ruffled than usual. She felt a flare inside her, fierce and instantaneous, as that thought in turn reminded her of Karin.

For, as she'd driven in through the gates of the mansion, who had driven past her, heading for the exit? None other than Karin, eyes fixed straight in front of her, steadfastly ignoring her, just as she had before.

I see, Sally had thought, her insides curling uncomfortably. This love-affair is obviously still flourishing. Quite clearly, Karin had just spent the night with Josh.

She'd tried to tell herself as she parked the car that all she felt was disapproval at the shameless way Josh flaunted his women. But she knew now that wasn't so. As she stared at his ruffled hair and fought to quell the flare it had provoked inside her, she knew that what she was feeling was something she ought not to be feeling.

I'm jealous, she thought, appalled at the idea. Why on earth should I be jealous?

'So, I've got a nerve, have I?' Josh cut through her thoughts. 'Oh, well,' he smiled, 'you're not the first to tell me that.'

'No doubt I'm not—and I don't know why you're smiling.'

Sally looked back at him, poker-faced. Get yourself together, she was telling herself. First goosebumps, now silly jealousy. What the devil's going on?

She threw him a dagger look. 'It wasn't meant to be a compliment.'

'No?' His smile widened. 'What a disappointment.'

'I'll bet.' Sally eyed him, resisting the urge to smile back. That smile of his really could be disarmingly infectious! 'However, I'm sure you can live without my compliments,' she added.

'Well, I've managed up until now.' Josh continued to smile at her. 'You've never been exactly liberal with your compliments.'

'I've never found anything to compliment.'

'Quite so.' Josh held her eyes.

'And, besides, there've always been plenty of others to make up for my lack of generosity. And I'm sure there still are,' Sally elaborated for good measure, wishing she hadn't found herself thinking of Karin as she said it. 'You always did like to surround yourself with admirers.'

As he simply shook his dark head and continued to smile, Sally thrust her hands impatiently into the pockets of her jeans.

'I'll bet you don't keep other people—your admirers,' she clarified tetchily, 'hanging around waiting for half an hour?'

'Special treatment for a special case.'

'Hah! In that case, I suppose I should be grateful that you only kept me waiting for half an hour! I suppose I should consider myself lucky you deigned to see me at all!'

Josh's expression had subtly altered. He was no longer smiling. 'I'd reserve judgement on that, if I were you, until our meeting is over. By then,' he added, smiling a cold smile, 'you may not be feeling quite so lucky.'

He held her eyes a moment before swivelling round and reaching for one of the phones on the desk. 'Coffee and toast?' he asked her. 'Are you sure that's all you want?'

Sally nodded. 'That will be fine.' What had he meant, she was wondering, by that 'You may not be feeling quite so lucky'? It was a grim reminder of that other battle they were locked in—the one concerning the future of her shop—and it had sounded uncomfortably like a threat.

As he punched in some numbers and spoke to the housekeeper, Sally watched him warily beneath her lashes. Was he planning to spring yet another surprise on her? Maybe he'd brought the date of her eviction forward?

As a spurt of panic touched her she took a deep breath and inwardly willed herself to remain calm and in control. She had promised herself last night that she would tell him about the necklace, for that, she still felt certain, was at the root of everything.

Convincing him wouldn't be easy. After all, she had no proof. She would simply have to rely on her powers of persuasion. And her powers of anything seemed to desert her somewhat when she was confronted with Josh!

He was laying down the phone. 'Your breakfast's on its way.' Then he turned to face her fully. 'Do you mind eating it in here, or would you prefer moving to the breakfast-room?'

'Here's fine.' Such civility. Such thoughtfulness. Such caring. He'd always been good at faking such qualities. That was part of his power, part of his charm. But underneath, of course, and especially where she was concerned, he didn't give a tinker's damn. The truth was, he'd probably rather enjoy seeing her choke on this breakfast he'd so courteously gone to the trouble of ordering.

'Good.' He remained propped on the edge of the desk. 'Why don't you take a seat?' He waved at one of the chairs. 'Make yourself comfortable. After all,' he added, 'I suspect you're probably going to be here for some time.'

Sally had assumed that from the start—though she hoped she'd be finished by lunchtime, when Clive was due to arrive back. That was why she'd phoned Sharon and asked her to look after the shop.

So, the sooner she got started, the better. As she crossed to the chair, she caught Josh's eye. 'Before we start, I have something I want to tell you——'

'What do you think of my office?'

He had cut through her deliberately. And as he'd spoken, he had risen suddenly to his feet, so that for a moment they stood facing one another, only a couple of feet apart.

Sally started, feeling her breath catch. All her muscles seemed to stiffen. She looked into his face, helpless emotion flooding through her. The blood was thundering in her ears.

'I——' she said. Her tongue had turned to cardboard. His nearness filled her senses, overwhelming her, sending a panic of sweet longing sweeping through her.

'Aunt Mimi was good enough to give me the use of this room. Perhaps you remember—it used to be one of the minor drawing-rooms.' He was smiling, a strange smile, the black eyes boring through her. 'We used to be allowed to play here when it was raining.'

'I remember.'

'Happy days, eh?'

'Yes, they were happy.'

As she said it, another rush of longing poured through her. A longing for things past. Or for what might have been. She wasn't sure. All she knew was that there was a sudden ache inside her. Unable to conceal it, she dropped her eyes to the floor.

She heard Josh say, 'What a pity such things have to end.'

'Yes, it is.'

Sally continued to stare at the carpet. And what a pity they had to end in such an ugly fashion, she was thinking, somehow tainting all the happiness that had gone before.

As she thought that, she suddenly remembered there was something she had to tell him. She looked up into his face again. But she couldn't remember what it was. Josh was looking down at her with a look of such intensity that for a moment she was incapable of thinking anything at all.

The feeling didn't pass until he took a step away from her and, still watching her, seated himself in one of the leather-backed chairs.

Sally sank into the seat opposite him, her legs like water, as he told her, continuing their conversation, 'It's useful, having this room. Even though I don't spend a lot of time here, when I am here I usually need to do a bit of business. Fortunately, Aunt Mimi has always been most tolerant about these things.'

Sally nodded. 'Of course.' Aunt Mimi doted on Josh.

She cast a quick glance round, her eyes seeing nothing, but suddenly desperate to detach her gaze from his and dispel the emotions that that brief trip

into the past had so suddenly and so violently un-
leashed in her. She didn't look back at him until
she felt in control once again.

'You must be very busy.' Her tone was controlled. 'I mean, if you have to keep working even
when you're on holiday.'

'It's not really working. Only the occasional
phone call.' Josh paused for an instant and smiled
amusedly. 'And, of course, the occasional quick
check with the computer.'

'Of course.' Sally nodded, her tone ironical. 'The
occasional quick check with the computer that
forces you to keep people waiting.'

Saying that finally dispelled all her vulnerable
feelings. She straightened in her chair. 'So why am
I here? Kindly explain the dramatic summons.'

It was at that moment that there was a sharp tap
at the door.

'Come in, Mrs Lowe!' Josh rose to his feet and
crossed to the door to usher in the housekeeper.

The woman cast a smile at Sally as she came in
bearing a laden tray. Then she turned to Josh. 'I
made enough coffee for two,' she told him, 'just in
case you felt like a cup.'

'Good woman. I reckon I do.' Josh relieved her
of the tray and laid it down on the cluttered desk.
'You always were an expert at anticipating my
needs.'

And you always were an expert in the charm de-
partment, Sally observed to herself, flicking him a
look, as Mrs Lowe beamed broadly at the compliment. He had always known how to make Aunt
Mimi's housekeepers beam!

'Eat up, then.' As, still beaming, the house-keeper departed, Josh reseated himself opposite Sally. 'And perhaps,' he added, 'while you're about it, you wouldn't mind pouring me a cup of that delicious-smelling coffee.'

'Not in the slightest.' Sally turned to the tray beside her, lifted the silver coffee-pot and poured two cups. Then, without thinking what she was doing, she poured a dash of cream into one of them, stirred in a spoonful of sugar and held it out to Josh.

'You remembered.' He held her eyes as he took the cup from her. 'Fancy that. I'm most impressed.'

'Don't be. It doesn't mean anything.' But as she said it she jerked her eyes away, aware of the warm flush that had crept up her neck. For it had struck Sally, too, as she'd handed him the cup, that she'd remembered how he took his coffee without even having to think about it. She felt a little put out. It seemed inappropriately cosy.

She said, carefully casual, 'My brain is full of all sorts of meaningless junk. That was just one very small example.'

In response, continuing to watch her over the top of the cup, Josh took a mouthful of his coffee. Then, it seemed to Sally, just to annoy her, he observed, before laying the cup down again, 'And you've got it just right. Just the right amount of cream and sugar. I find most people tend to overdo it.'

Sally thinned her lips at him. 'I thought we were here for a purpose ... I mean other than discussing how you like your coffee.'

'Indeed we are.' His eyes flitted over her. And it was not a casual glance. He seemed to be studying her.

Sally forced herself to look back at him, conquering her discomfort. And suddenly she remembered what she'd been planning to tell him. She sat forward in her seat, cleared her throat and began, 'There's something I would like to——'

'Your toast will be getting cold.' Again he interrupted her. 'Eat up. It's better when it's warm.'

Sally sighed and turned automatically towards the tray. Then she shook herself inwardly. She would not be put off. Taking a deep breath, she turned to him.

'Look——' she began.

But that was as far as she got. She had frozen in her seat, shocked by the suddenly harsh expression on his face. His eyes, all at once, were as black as thunderclouds.

'Do you know what this is?' He gestured with his eyes to the blue pottery owl he held in one hand. His tone was as rough as shattered granite.

Sally stared fixedly at the owl, a frown on her face. She shifted her gaze to look at him. 'Yes,' she said.

'And what is it?'

'It's an owl. A pottery owl.' What a silly question. Anyone could see that.

Josh continued to look at her, ignoring her sarcasm. A moment passed. Then he said, 'And whose work is it?'

Sally knew the answer to that, too. She had recognised the owl instantly. Yet she hesitated just a moment before answering, 'It's Karin's.' The sight of the owl and the return to the subject of Karin had sent a sword-thrust of foolish resentment stabbing through her.

Josh had caught her hesitation, and now he proceeded to misinterpret it. 'I'm glad you resisted the temptation to deny all knowledge. If nothing else, that should save us a bit of time.'

What was he talking about? Sally frowned at him. 'Why on earth should I deny it?' Then her frown grew deeper. 'And what has Karin's owl got to do with anything?'

'Such innocence.' Now it was Josh's turn to be sarcastic. He laid down the owl on the leather-tooled desk-top, sat back in his chair and smiled a hangman's smile. 'You said you wanted to know why I've decided to close your business.' His eyes glinted with malice. 'That owl is the reason.'

Sally was none the wiser. He was talking in riddles. He was also acting inconsistently. She proceeded to point this out to him.

She reached for a piece of toast as calmly as she was able—that smile on his face had unnerved her a little—and observed as she spread it lightly with butter, 'I thought you'd refused to discuss your reasons until Clive was here.' She flicked Josh a cool look from beneath her lashes. 'Something about saving time, you said.'

'Yes, that was what I'd intended.' He took another mouthful of his coffee, without for a moment detaching his eyes from hers. 'But, unfortunately, I've been forced to change my plans. I don't have time to waste hanging around waiting for someone who isn't going to show.'

Sally took a bite of her toast. 'Don't be so impatient,' she told him. 'Clive's due back today at lunchtime. You won't have long to wait.' She half turned to reach out for her coffee-cup. 'So all this sudden urgency is really a bit silly. You may as well wait another couple of hours.'

It was at that precise moment that she nearly choked on her toast. Something went whizzing past her head and landed with a thud in the wall to her right. Sally whirled round, her heart racing. 'What the devil was that?'

What she saw was a dartboard that she hadn't noticed before, with, still quivering in its centre, a red-feathered dart. She spun round to scowl at Josh. 'Are you trying to kill me?' she accused.

'If I were trying to kill you, I'd aim at you and not at the dartboard, which happens to be in an entirely different line of fire.' Steely-eyed, as though warning her that he could always change his mind, he took another dart from the wooden box on the desk—something else that Sally hadn't noticed!— and sent it whizzing past her to land in the dartboard, dead centre.

Sally glared at the dartboard and then at him. 'I'm surprised you haven't got my picture pasted up there! That would account for your perfect aim.'

He smiled at that. 'Perhaps I do usually. Perhaps I took it down just before you came.'

'In order to spare my feelings.' Sally grimaced. 'How unlikely.' But though it was she who had made the suggestion in the first place, she rather disliked the possibility that it might just be true!

Josh was holding up another dart. 'So, what were you saying? About Clive... Something about expecting him home today...?'

'Yes, that's what I said. He'll be back by lunchtime.'

Josh shook his head. 'Try again,' he said.

'What do you mean?' Sally scowled. 'What do you mean try again?'

'I mean try again, and this time try the truth.' The shiny steel dart glinted ominously in his hand. 'I'm not in the mood for listening to lies.'

'Why should I lie?' Sally stared at the dart. It looked marginally less lethal than the look in his eyes. 'I told you Clive will be back by lunchtime.'

The dart left his hand and whizzed in a blur past her. Sally jumped nervously as, with a thud, it hit the board. But she didn't bother to check if it was another bull's-eye. Somehow, almost eerily, she knew that it was.

But he was way off the mark with that strange accusation. She repeated, 'By lunchtime. That's what he told me on the phone last night.'

Josh stood up suddenly, making her jump again. Then, snatching up the blue pottery owl from the desk-top, he stepped towards her and thrust it at her.

'Read what's written on the bottom of that.'

As Sally took it, startled, he stepped past her to the dartboard and in one ferocious movement removed the three darts. Dark eyes watching her, he stood over her. 'Read out loud what it says.'

It was difficult to focus with him standing over her. One hard muscular thigh was only inches from her elbow. She was suddenly filled with the fear of brushing against it.

But she swallowed hard and pulled herself together. She was behaving like a silly, immature eleven-year-old.

'It says Polly Ong.' She raised her eyes to his, then dropped them away sharply as his gaze seemed to burn through her. 'I was obviously mistaken. It's not Karin's, after all.'

Josh laughed then, a sound that chilled her to the marrow. 'No, you were not mistaken, as you perfectly well know.' As he spoke, he snatched the pottery bird from her fingers. 'This owl could be no one's work but Karin's.'

'That's what I thought at first... It's very similar to one we had for sale recently in the shop. But it says Polly Ong.' He had moved away a little and she was finding it easier to breathe now. 'They obviously have very similar styles.'

For some reason, that remark seemed to have the effect of enraging him. He swung round once more to face her. 'Don't sit there and lie to me! Do you think I'm an idiot? I know what's going on!'

'Well, that's more than I do!' Sally sprang to her feet. Suddenly, she'd had enough of being pushed around verbally, not to mention having darts sent whizzing past her ear! 'I don't know anything about your owl or who made it! I don't know who Polly Ong is and, quite frankly, I don't care! And I wish you'd just tell me what the hell you're trying to say to me!'

'I'll tell you what I'm trying to say to you, you little cheat, you little liar...!' Josh grabbed her by the wrist and snatched her closer, thrusting the blue pottery owl in her face. 'This mark here, this signature, Polly Ong, has been superimposed upon the original one. It's hard to see it with the naked eye, but I can assure you that the original mark was KS—Karin's signature, as you know.'

As he shook her, Sally blurted, 'Yes, I know that.' Suddenly, she was finding it hard to co-ordinate. She could feel his arm against her arm, his thigh against her thigh and the sweet warm touch of his breath in her hair. And, suddenly, she was incapable of concentrating on anything else.

He was no longer holding on to her, but she might as well have been handcuffed. In a way, she almost wished she were. It would have explained the reason why she hadn't moved a muscle. She would have been able to blame it on him.

But she couldn't. For some reason she was standing there voluntarily, breathing in the warmth of him, feeling it stir her, her heart suddenly bucking like a wild thing in her breast.

It was madness and it terrified her, but she couldn't shake the feeling off.

Then, through the clamour in her head, she heard him say Clive's name. 'So do you still maintain,' he was saying, 'that he'll be back by lunchtime?'

Sally felt shame rush through her. What was she thinking of? Clive was her boyfriend. The man who wanted to marry her. The man she might end up spending her life with.

And here she was lusting after a man she hated and who wished her and Clive nothing but harm. For she had been lusting. There was no other way to put it. That twanging in her loins had been raw, animal lust.

She took a step back, filled with horror at herself, and somehow managed to answer Josh's question. 'Of course I do,' she answered huskily. She cleared her throat quickly. 'He'll be home by lunch today.'

'No, he won't, and you know it!' Josh had stepped away contemptuously. Had his eyes been scissors they'd have cut her to pieces. 'He won't be back. Certainly not today. I know as well as you do that your dear Clive has done a runner.'

Sally blinked at him. 'Done a runner? Why on earth would he do that?'

'Because he knows I'm on to the two of you. No doubt you told him. With his record it makes sense that he'd prefer to make himself scarce for a while— even though it means leaving you to take all the heat.'

'I don't know what you're talking about.' Sally sank down on to her chair again. Suddenly the effort of following this conversation was exhausting. 'I wish you'd start saying something that makes some sense.'

Josh threw her a shrewd look. He clearly thought she was bluffing. 'OK,' he conceded, once more seating himself opposite her. 'Let's try some simple, straightforward little facts and see if you can understand those.'

He held up the blue pottery owl in front of her. 'Tell me how much one of these would cost.'

Sally thought for a moment. 'I'm not a hundred-per-cent sure. Clive's the pottery expert, not me. But I seem to remember that one we had in the shop was tagged at about fifteen or sixteen pounds.'

'That sounds reasonable.'

So, she'd got something right! Involuntarily, a relieved smile touched Sally's lips.

But it didn't linger long. Josh leaned towards her. 'So how come this one was on sale down in London for a figure approaching ten times that amount?'

'Ten times that amount?'

'Don't look so surprised. You know very well that's how much these owls fetch down there.'

Sally knew no such thing. In fact, at that precise moment, she wasn't even sure she knew her own name. She stared at Josh in silence as he continued, 'Imagine poor Karin's astonishment and dismay when she walked into a craft shop near where I live and saw her work on sale, under another name, at prices way beyond anything she's ever been paid for it. I'm sure you can appreciate that she was rather upset.'

Sally stared at him. Amid everything he had just told her, one single, fiercely disturbing point stood out. Tonelessly, she said, 'A craft shop near where you live?'

'That's right. Near Regent's Park.'

She already knew where he lived. She frowned. 'What was Karin doing in Regent's Park?'

One black eyebrow lifted. 'She was staying with me. Not that I see what difference that makes.'

It shouldn't make any difference. But, all the same, it did. This affair with Karin, it was suddenly painfully clear to Sally, was not just a fleeting, new attachment, after all.

She found herself asking, 'And when was all this?'

'You mean when did Karin make this discovery? A few weeks ago. And, not surprisingly, she's been devastated ever since.'

A little like I feel, Sally found herself thinking, knowing she should be thinking no such thing. Her brain was churning, trying to sort out what he'd told her, trying not think of Regent's Park and the flat there where Karin had stayed.

'Maybe they're not her owls.' She forced herself to say something. He was watching her, waiting for her reaction. 'I mean, if, like that blue one, they're signed Polly Ong, maybe they're not Karin's, maybe they're Polly Ong's.' She frowned, wishing Clive were there. He knew all about pottery. 'Maybe this Polly Ong is someone famous. She must be—or at least she's popular—to command such prices.'

Josh said nothing for a moment. His eyes pierced right through her. He was not impressed, she could tell, by her perfectly rational suggestion.

His tone was clipped as he told her. 'Yes, she is indeed popular. But there is no Polly Ong. And the owls are Karin's.'

'How can you be sure of that? Maybe you're wrong about the name being changed.'

'Stop bluffing, Sally.'

'I'm not bluffing! I'm just trying to find an explanation as to how some owls that look a lot like Karin's could end up in London being sold for a small fortune under somebody else's name! And the most likely explanation I can think of is that they are in fact somebody else's!'

Josh leaned towards her suddenly, making her jump back. 'An artist knows her own work. She doesn't make mistakes like that. Karin saw the owls and recognised them instantly. She held them in her hand and she *knew* that they were hers. There wasn't even a flicker of doubt in her mind.'

He narrowed his dark eyes, fixing Sally in her seat. 'Would you have any doubts as to the identity of one your paintings? Even if you found one of them signed Polly Ong...' He paused, letting the irony in his voice flow over her. 'Even then, surely, you'd know the painting was yours?'

'Of course I would.' Sally glanced down at the floor. That was something she could not argue with. Others might mistake her work, but she never would. Every daub, every brush-stroke of every painting she'd ever done was tattooed permanently on her brain.

She sighed. 'And is Karin absolutely sure?'

But as she raised her eyes to Josh's a cold chill stole through her. Never had she seen so much contempt on anyone's face.

He did not answer her and his silence was terrible. Sally felt as though her soul was being crushed beneath its weight. Then, as though seeking to control the emotions within him, very slowly, not looking at her, he aimed a dart at the dartboard.

'You know, when Aunt Mimi told me about the shop,' he told her, as with a thud the dart connected with the cork, 'I admired your initiative. It seemed a laudible idea to support yourself with a little craft shop while continuing to paint seriously in your spare time...'

He cast her a rough glance. 'I have got the story right?' A second dart thudded into the dartboard. 'That was what you told Aunt Mimi when you ap-

proached her, wasn't it? That was the story we were
all supposed to believe?'

Sally swallowed drily. What was coming now?
She nodded. 'And that was—that *is*—the truth,'
she said.

'I think not.' Josh's tone was ominously quiet.
He held the third dart poised in his hand. 'I think
the shop was just a convenient cover for your dishonest goings-on. You teamed up with Clive—well,
he was the perfect accomplice, wasn't he? Plenty
of previous experience in that sort of thing—and
proceeded to find yourself some talented young
craftspeople whose work you could sell at a large
profit up in London while pretending to sell it for
a pittance down here.'

As he paused to draw a breath, it was as though
the very room shook. 'But I shouldn't be surprised.' His eyes were like lances. 'You always had
leanings in that direction . . .'

'No!' As Sally leapt to her feet to defend herself,
the dart whizzed past her ear, shocking her into
silence.

Josh took a step towards her, his eyes blazing
down at her. 'But there'll be no more stealing, no
more cheating! Your career is over! I intend to put
a stop to you—you and that filthy boyfriend of
yours! Do you understand?' He stood there blazing
down at her, all the wrath of hell pouring down at
her from his eyes. 'You've always been a thief, and
now you're going to pay for it!'

And that was when Sally could bear his taunts
no longer. She flew at him bodily, screeching like
a banshee.

CHAPTER FIVE

'I WON'T allow you to say these things about me! I'm not a thief! I never have been!'

Sally had flung herself against him and was beating him with her fists, tears of anger and frustration starting from her eyes. 'You have no right to say these awful things about me!'

'No? You're completely innocent, are you?' Josh merely smiled a scathing smile as her blows rained down harmlessly against his arms and chest. 'The wronged innocent? Oh, yes, I'm sure to believe that.'

'It's true! I swear to you!' She seized him by the shirt-front, wrenching and pulling as though she would tear the shirt from his body. 'How can you believe such awful things of me?'

As she looked into his face, pain and desperation in her eyes, she thought about the necklace and how she'd planned to tell him the true story. But what would be the point of doing that now?

This was not about the necklace. This was about something far more sinister. She was being accused of the worst kind of treachery and dishonesty. She was being accused of betraying and exploiting her fellow-artists. And the very idea was utterly appalling.

She tugged futilely at his shirt-front. 'None of what you've said is true! Why are you accusing me of all those make-believe crimes?'

'Take my word for it, there's nothing make-believe about them.' Josh had caught hold of her by the wrists, lightly, to stem her assault on him. Suddenly, remarkably calm, he looked down into her eyes. 'Why did you do it, Sally? You were such a nice kid when you were younger. How could you let your family down this way?'

'My family?'

Sally blinked at him, sudden confusion pouring through her. The gentle way he was holding her and the way he was looking down at her, with something close to warmth and caring in his eyes, all at once was sending shivers through her.

She longed to fall against him, to beg him to believe her, to feel his arms slide comfortingly around her, holding her close, his warmth flooding through her, sustaining her, cleansing her of this ugliness he believed.

His hands had slid up from her wrists to hold her by the arms, and his grip, though firm, was light and gentle. A sincere look filled his eyes. He frowned a little. 'Your family are good and decent people. Don't you care that they'd be devastated if they knew?'

'Of course I care. But they don't know, do they?'

Sally felt a tightening within her as she thought of her parents, both gone now from the village to live and work in Somerset, and of the aunts and cousins who still lived round about. She would never survive the shame if any of them got to hear of this.

But Josh was shaking his head. 'I hope they needn't ever know. Your mother in particular. She doesn't deserve such a blow. Your mother is one of the most admirable women I've ever known.'

'I know.' And she knew also that Josh had spoken sincerely. He had his faults, he could be arrogant and overbearing, but he had always treated her mother with respect and kindness. She'd never realised it before, but she was grateful to him for that.

'So why did you do it?' He shook her gently. 'Surely a few hundred pounds, even a few thousand, isn't worth bringing yourself and your family into disrepute for?'

The way he was looking at her was making her heart spurt inside her. Sally hadn't seen that look in his eyes for years. She'd forgotten how warm and caring he could be—like on that long-ago day when he'd taught her to play table tennis!

One hand released her arm and reached up to tilt her chin. 'What happened, Sally? Was it that man who made you do it?'

Sally swallowed. 'What man?' Her mind had gone blank. She could think of nothing but the fingers that softly held her chin, sending darts of electricity glancing across her skin. She loved the feel of those long, strong fingers. She licked her dry lips. 'What man?' she said again.

'Clive. Was it Clive who talked you into this?'

'He didn't talk me into anything.'

'Don't keep denying it, Sally.' His finger stroked her cheek, making her shiver deliciously. The caress of his finger was soothing, hypnotic. 'Just tell me it was that man . . . that it was Clive who talked you into it, and I'll understand and we can put the whole thing behind us. Remember, I know what kind of man Clive is. You're not the first one he's led astray.'

Sally frowned. She was confused. Why did he keep saying these things about Clive? She looked into his eyes. 'What do you mean?' she asked him. 'What do you mean, I'm not the first one he's led astray? What did you mean when you said earlier that he had a record?'

'Didn't you know?'

'Know what?'

'About his record.'

'Of course I didn't know. He hasn't got one!'

'I suppose you're right, he hasn't. He got off on a technicality. But he was guilty. Even his own lawyer had no doubts about that. He did the burglary. He and his friend.'

'What are you talking about?' This conversation was getting ridiculous. And, more than just ridiculous, Sally found it threatening and frightening. He had a nerve saying all these terrible things about Clive!

Suddenly coming to her senses, she snatched herself free from him. 'What you're saying is slander! I won't listen to another word of it!'

'How very noble and loyal of you.' Josh's expression had suddenly hardened. 'Normally, I would find such sentiments admirable, but in this instance, I'm afraid, I find them rather sickening. Such loyalty to a criminal ought to be beneath you, Sally.'

'Why, since I'm a criminal, too? Surely nothing could be more natural? We criminals have to stick together!'

'Loyalty among thieves? There's no such thing, Sally. Stick with that man and you'll soon find that out.'

'I intend sticking with him!'

Suddenly, she was angry and defiant. She didn't care what Josh thought. The whole thing was preposterous!

She swung away from him. 'I've had enough of this nonsense. If you've finished with me, I'd like to leave now!'

As she snatched up her bag, Josh was blocking her exit. 'Oh, I haven't finished with you. Not by a long shot.' His eyes bored into her, black and menacing. 'To be truthful, I haven't even started with you yet.'

Sally felt a coldness touch her. She could see he really meant it. Josh had never really been her friend, but now, implacably, he was her enemy.

Still, she forced herself to face him. 'So, what are you going to do with me? Are you going to have me drawn and quartered and my head put on a stake?'

'Nothing quite so theatrical.' Josh smiled a grim smile. 'All I intend to do is put an end to your trickery—and, of course, extract from you the money you've stolen and hand it over to its rightful owner.' As she glared at him, he added, 'For the sake of your parents, I hope to do it all without involving the police. Although, if it weren't for them, I wouldn't think twice. It would give me the greatest pleasure to see you put behind bars.'

Nice thought! Sally shivered at the coldness of his words. Then she started as he moved suddenly. But all he was doing was stepping side.

'You may go,' he told her. 'That's all. For the moment.'

Sally stepped past him quickly and almost ran to the door. Then in the doorway she suddenly stopped and turned to look at him. 'How come you're so sure that I'm involved in all of this?' The thought had suddenly struck her. He seemed so certain.

He delivered her a long look. 'Oh, I'm certain,' he told her. 'I have an exact description of you from the shopkeeper in Regent's Park. He remembers you vividly from when you delivered the first lot of owls.' Josh smiled at her. 'You were unwise. You ought to have worn a disguise. That blonde hair of yours is very striking.'

Then he turned away abruptly, dismissing her. 'Now go. And, don't worry, I'll be in touch.' He cast her a predatory smile over his shoulder. 'As I told you, I haven't finished with you yet.'

It was late, almost midnight, and Sally was in her studio, dabbing ineffectually at the painting on the easel. But it was a waste of time. She couldn't concentrate. She tossed aside her brush and sank down on her stool.

One of the things that bothered her most was that there was no sign of Clive. Lunchtime had come and gone long ago and he hadn't turned up. He hadn't even phoned.

It was most distressing. She'd passed the day on tenterhooks.

'Are you sure there wasn't a phone call this morning?' she asked Sharon, at least a dozen times throughout the day. For it wasn't like Clive. It wasn't like him at all. He always phoned if he was going to be late.

But this time he hadn't. And there was just no sign of him. Sally had called his flat at least a score of times, leaving messages on his answering machine. But, so far at least, he hadn't called back.

After she'd shut up the shop, she'd driven to his flat and rung the bell endlessly and even spoken to the neighbours. But no one had seen him and the flat was dark and silent. It was perfectly clear he wasn't there.

That was when she had started to panic a little. What if there'd been an accident? A car crash or something? So she phoned the police and asked them to check if there'd been an accident anywhere along the route he'd be taking back to the village.

To her relief, they told her no. But though she was relieved she was none the wiser. Where on earth had Clive disappeared to, and why?

Unable to eat dinner, she'd phoned the bed and breakfast where Clive normally stayed when he was travelling on business round the region.

'Yes, he was here,' the woman told her. 'But he checked out last night.' And no, he hadn't said where he was going.

So where did she go from here? Don't panic, Sally told herself. There's bound to be a perfectly rational explanation. He'll be in touch soon enough. Just keep calm. He's been tied up unexpectedly somewhere. It's as simple as that.

So she'd gone through to her studio and put on her smock and tried to do a bit of painting. That always calmed her down when she was anxious about something. But this time it didn't work. She just couldn't concentrate. Every second she was waiting, and praying, for the phone to ring.

Sally stared at it now as it sat there in defiant silence. 'Please ring! Come on, Clive! Let me know where you are!'

She sighed now and reached for the rag on the little table where she kept her jars of linseed oil and turps and distractedly wiped her discarded brush. The most difficult thing of all was shutting from her mind all the things Josh had said to her earlier about Clive.

'He won't be back,' he'd said. 'Clive has done a runner.'

That was nonsense, of course. What had Clive to run from? He was as innocent as she was in this whole crazy pantomime! Wherever Josh had got his story about Clive's supposed brush with the law from—that was, if he hadn't invented it himself!—it was pure and simple fantasy from start to finish!

Another thought struck her as she dropped her brush in the turps jar and set about wiping the paint from her palette knife. How could anyone have seen her at that shop in Regent's Park when she'd never been near Regent's Park in her life? The whole thing was a web of fabrication!

She laid down her palette knife and tossed the rag aside, then turned once more to gaze beseechingly at the telephone. Please ring, she begged silently. But it still paid no heed. It just sat there as silent as a tomb.

Sally glanced at her watch. She really ought to go to bed. There was no point in waiting up. She was utterly exhausted. And there was a phone at her bedside. She would hear it if it rang.

With a sigh she began to unbutton her smock. What a day it had been. One of the worst she could remember. Not only had she been told all sorts of lies about Clive and accused of crimes she had never committed, it had also been revealed to her that she apparently had a double who went around London besmirching her name!

At that thought she froze suddenly. Why hadn't it occurred to her sooner? With a yelp of excitement she leapt across the room, grabbed the phone book, leafed through it quickly and, holding her breath, dialled Josh's number.

The number connected instantly. She waited impatiently as it rang, holding the receiver tightly against her ear.

Then a sudden thought occurred to her as it continued to ring unanswered. Maybe Josh was with Karin. Making love to her. Maybe that was why he wasn't answering the phone.

Her heart lurched inside her. She almost laid down the phone. The thought of him with Karin had knocked the breath from her body.

But at that very moment he answered. 'Yes?' he said.

Again Sally almost laid the phone down. He sounded gruff and irritated. He *had* been making love to Karin, she thought bleakly. She's probably lying there all warm and naked beside him.

But as he repeated, more sharply, 'Yes? Who is it?' Sally forced herself to answer.

'It's me,' she said. 'Sally. I have a request to make ... I want to go with you to Regent's Park. As soon as possible. Tomorrow, if we can.'

'Is this a proposition?'

Sally could tell he was smiling. She wondered if Karin was smiling, too.

She clutched the receiver, struggling to banish these thoughts, forcing herself to concentrate on what she was saying. 'It's important. Will you take me? Please don't say no.'

There was a silence. Then Josh said, 'Come round to my place tomorrow morning and we can discuss what this is all about.'

Then, before she could say a word, the phone went dead.

Sally laid down the receiver, trying hard to feel excited. At least he seemed prepared to consider her request.

But all she could think about was that up at the mansion Josh and Karin were making love together in Josh's big four-poster bed.

'So, what's all this about, then? Kindly explain yourself.'

It was morning and Josh and Sally were out on the patio at the mansion, drinking coffee in the sunshine.

To Sally's relief, this morning she hadn't bumped into Karin. But then she'd arrived a little later than yesterday. Karin had had plenty of time to make her exit.

Sally glanced at Josh's hair now, as he waited for her to answer. Today it didn't look ruffled. He'd had time to comb it. But I bet it was ruffled last night when I phoned, she thought.

That thought was like a knife turning inside her. She pushed it from her, hating herself for thinking it, and forced herself to concentrate on what she'd come to tell him.

She said, sitting forward in her seat. 'I had a sudden thought. That man in the Regent's Park craft shop... I know you believe that whoever he met was me. But it wasn't. And it seems to me the best way to prove it is to go there and confront him face to face.'

To her dismay, Josh shook his head. 'I don't think that will be necessary. The man was absolutely sure it was you.'

'But he was wrong! It wasn't me! It must have been someone who looked like me!'

'Oh, she looked like you, all right.' His tone was sarcastic. 'Five feet five, honey-blonde hair, about eight and a half stone, blue or green eyes——'

'I don't have blue or green eyes,' Sally broke in triumphantly. 'I have green eyes. Very definitely green!'

'Well, he wasn't sure about the eyes...except that they were either blue or green. But he was very definite about the rest.' Josh smiled, amused. 'You made quite an impression.'

'It seems I did.' Sally glared right through his smile. 'Which is rather remarkable, considering I was never even there!'

'So you say.'

'I say it because I wasn't!' Sally shook her head impatiently. 'That description you've just given me... There are thousands—*tens* of thousands— of girls who look like that!'

'Agreed.' To her surprise, he nodded.

'So, you see, it needn't have been me! It's perfectly obvious it was just someone who looked like me!'

He nodded again, and Sally's heart squeezed inside her. Had she actually convinced him he might be wrong?

But then he shook his head. 'But tell me one thing... Are there tens of thousands of girls of that description who also happen to be called Sally Woodstock?'

As she blinked at him, he added, 'No, I can see you agree with me that in the realms of coincidence that would be pushing it a bit.'

Yes, it would. Sally was stunned. 'You mean he mentioned me by name?' This was definitely getting to be a bit spooky!

Josh nodded. 'Not only that, he also knew you were from the village. Apparently, you were quite chatty. You told him all about your flat and the shop.' He shook his head. 'Most unwise,' he advised her. 'If you're bent on pursuing a career of crime, you must learn to be a great deal more discreet. I'm surprised your friend Clive didn't give you a few tips.'

There was the usual cutting edge to his voice as he mentioned Clive, but, in spite of that, Sally sensed he was in a lighter mood today. He seemed less bent on confrontation.

Perhaps he had had a particularly enjoyable night with Karin, she thought, hating the way her blood froze inside her.

But again she pushed that thought away. She had more important things to think about!

Regarding him earnestly, she pleaded, 'Take me to the shop, let me meet the shop owner, and you'll soon see how wrong you are. Please. Surely even you want to get to the truth?'

'I know the truth already.' He was immovable. But before Sally could protest again he asked her, dark eyes watching her, 'So where's what's-his-name... your partner and boyfriend? Is he looking after the shop?'

He shot her a cutting look as he said that last bit and helped himself to a mouthful of coffee. He didn't believe for one minute that Clive had come back.

And, unfortunately, he was right. Though not for the reasons he'd suggested. Sally regarded him steadily. 'Clive hasn't come back.'

'Not come back?' Josh made a pretence at being astounded. 'Goodness. How very odd. I wonder what he's up to?'

'I shouldn't think he's up to anything. At least, not anything criminal. He's probably just been unavoidably delayed.'

'Unavoidably delayed. Yes, that sounds like it.' Josh flicked her a look of open amusement. 'How very thoughtless of him,' he added.

Sally glared at him. He was enjoying himself hugely. The black eyes danced like starlight on water. And though his amusement irked her, it also reassured her. Yesterday, he would not have made a joke of it. Yesterday, he'd have sent a dart whizzing past her ear! Today he might be a little more malleable.

She said, 'I'm sure he has a perfectly good explanation. These things happen. People get delayed——'

'Unavoidably.'

'Yes. Unavoidably.'

As he smiled, Josh reached up and ran a hand across his hair, ruffling it slightly, sending a jolt through Sally. And to her own utter astonishment and mild horror, as she stared at his ruffled hair, Sally heard herself say, 'How's Karin? I didn't see her this morning.'

Josh delivered her an odd look. Then, watching her, he answered, 'Karin, quite naturally, is feeling cheated and upset. She wants the money that's owed her.' He paused an instant. 'And I intend to see she gets it.'

There was just a little too much concern in his tone for comfort. Sally felt herself recoil a little. Then with an air of bravado she shot back at him, 'How touching. Sir Galahad to the rescue!'

Josh did not find that funny. 'So, you have the gall to make a joke of it? I'm afraid,' he rebuked her, 'I find that in rather poor taste.'

'It might be in bad taste if I were the guilty party!'

Sally felt crushed by the way he had leapt to defend Karin. He wasn't just sleeping with her. It sounded as though he really cared for her.

So what? she told herself. What do I care? She forced herself to hold his cold gaze and demanded, 'That's why we have to go to London! That's why we have to see this shopkeeper. He's the only one who can tell you it wasn't me!'

Josh regarded her for a long moment. The look on his face was unreadable.

'Please!' Sally protested. 'What have you got to lose?'

'Time, for one thing. And I hate to waste time.'

'But that's not a problem, if that's what you're worried about! We can do it in a day! Half a day! Half an hour! That guy in the shop will only have to look at me to know it wasn't me he met before!'

Josh seemed to be considering. His eyes pierced through her. Then he said in a quiet voice, 'But there was more to it than that.'

'More, how? What do you mean more?'

'The shopkeeper didn't just see you, he didn't just speak to you.' Josh paused. 'He also has your signature.'

'My what? What do you mean, he has my signature?'

'On various letters and agreements and things. He showed it to me. It was definitely your signature.'

Sally felt herself blanch. Her stomach heaved inside her. She sat back in her seat as though all the air had been let out of her.

'He can't have my signature,' she said in a weak voice. Suddenly, she felt like weeping.

'So, you see, the evidence against you is overwhelming.' Josh was rising to his feet. 'Your continued denials are pointless. I would never have accused you in the first place if I hadn't been certain.'

He turned to look at her. 'So I'm sorry to say I see no point in a trip to London. As I said, I hate to waste time.'

Sally felt as though the roof of the world was falling in on her. Shoulders bowed, suddenly bereft of the ability to speak, she stared numbly at Josh as he began to move away.

'So we're back where we started,' he was saying. 'The lease on the shop will not be renewed. I'm going to put you out of business.'

'Blow the business! Blow the shop!'

Suddenly unable to control herself, Sally was springing to her feet, sending the cane table sprawling headlong over the patio. There was a slow, splintering crash as hand-decorated Limoges coffee-cups disintegrated into tiny pieces over the tiles.

But Sally was oblivious. 'I don't care about the shop! What I care about is my reputation! I can't let this go on—people thinking I'm a criminal! I won't let it go on! I demand the right to clear my name!'

Josh was standing very still, his gaze fixed on her unblinkingly. He's going to tear me apart now, Sally thought with a shiver.

But she didn't care. She didn't regret her outburst. The only regret she had was that she hadn't made it sooner.

'So there,' she added for good measure, her sea-green eyes sparking with defiance. 'I demand that you take me to London immediately!'

There was another silent pause as Josh continued to watch her. She'd blown it, Sally thought dismally. He'd never agree now.

And, as he half turned to continue his exit from the patio, her heart felt as though it had dropped into her shoes. All was lost. She would be branded a thief forever.

But then, quite suddenly, he stopped and turned to look at her. And, though his expression was unfathomable, his words were plain enough.

'Go home and prepare an overnight bag. I'll pick you up after lunch. We're going to London.'

Back home in her little flat, Sally threw some things into a bag. Whatever came to hand. She barely noticed. All she knew was that her heart was singing inside her, with relief and joy and irrepressible excitement. He had consented, after all! She would be able to prove her innocence!

And she could still scarcely believe it was really happening as, just before two, she climbed into the red Ferrari. Soon this nightmare would be over. At last, she would have the chance to clear her name!

But there was another thought, too, that snaked its way around her consciousness as the low, powerful car ate up the miles like spaghetti. She was going to the Regent's Park flat, where Karin had stayed. In spite of herself, she felt a dart of triumph.

For though it should have mattered not one jot that, even if only a little, she was evening up the score with Karin—after all, it was ludicrous that she was thinking in terms of scores, anyway!—the truth was that it gave Sally a decidedly warm feeling each time she dwelt upon where she was heading.

And the nearer they got, the warmer the sensation.

As the first glimpse of the greenery of Regent's Park came into view, Sally was positively glowing!

CHAPTER SIX

A FEW minutes later the red Ferrari swept up in front of one of the elegant Nash terraces overlooking Regent's Park. Wow, Sally was thinking, this is living!

Then, astonished and delighted at the opulence that greeted her, she was following Josh into a chandeliered hallway and stepping into a spacious, silent lift. Josh's apartment was on the top floor. The penthouse—what else? A moment later they were inside. Sally's jaw dropped.

'This is incredible. I had no idea you lived like this!' Sally was unable to stop the spontaneous compliment. She looked around her in admiration. 'This really is superb.'

'Do you like it?' But there was no false modesty in the question.

Sally met his smile and laughed. 'What's not to like?'

She followed him into the drawing-room with its splendid furniture—a clever, subtle mix of antique and modern—and stepped to the window with its view over the park. Then she turned and smiled at him over her shoulder. 'I don't mind telling you I'm very impressed.'

'I'm glad you approve.' He was standing watching her. 'As I've often told you, I admire your taste.'

Sally couldn't resist a smile. 'That's because it coincides with yours.' Then she added, teasing him a little, 'As I've often told you.'

Josh smiled back at her. 'Yes, you're right. We do seem to have had a lot of our conversations before. That's because we go back a long way.'

As he held her eyes, Sally felt her heart turn over. I've known him longer than I've known most people in my life, she was thinking. He is part of my life. Inextricably.

The thought made her smile a bittersweet smile. She held Josh's eyes. 'Perhaps,' she suggested, 'we're destined to be a permanent thorn in each other's sides.'

She had said it without rancour. Josh nodded. 'Perhaps.' And for a moment he continued to hold her eyes. Then he stepped towards the bell-pull on the wall behind him. 'I suggest we have a coffee,' he said, giving it a tug, 'before we do... anything else.'

How nicely he had phrased that, and so considerately, as though he was loath to spoil the mood between them. But, all the same, Sally felt a sudden dart of anxiety. The 'anything else' he'd been referring to was the visit to the craft shop that she'd finally managed to talk him into.

Though I have no cause to feel anxious, she reminded herself quickly. All that could happen now was that her innocence would be proved.

A moment later, on silent feet, a middle-aged man appeared. 'You rang, sir?' As he addressed Josh, Sally had to hide a smile. This man was obviously Josh's butler—and he couldn't have looked more like a butler if he'd tried!

'We'd like some coffee, please, Roberts.' Josh flicked a glance at Sally. 'Unless, of course, you'd prefer tea?'

'No, coffee's fine.' Sally nodded her assent. Then she crossed to one of the gold brocade-covered armchairs that stood by the window and seated herself in it.

She almost wished she hadn't! It was so deep and soft she almost disappeared from view!

Sally drew herself up a little as Roberts the butler withdrew, and glanced at Josh who had slipped off his jacket and was tossing it down on to the arm of a nearby sofa.

'So, where is this craft shop?' she ventured, struggling to surface from the sea of cushions. 'Is it near here? Will it take us long to get there?'

For a moment his eyes narrowed and a dark looked touched them, making Sally regret having brought up the subject. She'd been enjoying the oasis of civility between them.

Then suddenly he shrugged and smiled as he told her, 'It's a ten-minute walk or a twenty-minute drive. The traffic in London, I'm afraid, is a killer.'

Sally smiled back at him, relieved at this show of humour. So, their oasis of civility wasn't ruined after all. Then she settled herself more comfortably in the depths of her armchair and glanced around the room with interest.

'That's a lovely collection of paintings you've got,' she told him. It was the first thing that had struck her when she'd walked into the room. 'Did you inherit them from your parents?'

Josh had seated himself in one of the armchairs across from her—but, unlike Sally, had not disappeared! On the contrary, he fairly dominated the gold brocade.

He said in an even tone, 'I inherited nothing from my parents. Nothing, that is, other than debts.'

Sally remembered then and blushed to her hair roots with embarrassment. She had never known the details—they were none of her business—but she recalled her mother telling her, when Josh's parents died five years ago, killed together in a speedboat accident, that they'd left behind them a rather embarrassing legacy. They had not been the wealthy jet-setters they'd appeared to be. In fact, they'd been up to their ears in debt.

'I'm sorry.' She shook her head now. 'That was thoughtless and indiscreet.'

But Josh seemed unperturbed. He shrugged his shoulders lightly as he unbuttoned his shirt-cuffs and pushed back his sleeves. 'It doesn't matter. It doesn't bother me.' He smiled a wry smile. 'It all happened a long time ago. I've got over the shock.'

But there was something in his smile then, something fleeting but vivid, that seemed to reach out and pluck at Sally's heart-strings. It was that hint of regret she had seen so often when he spoke about his parents. It had been there nearly always. Even when he was a boy.

She felt moved by it to a degree that surprised her a little. She smiled back at him, feeling awkward. 'Yes, I suppose so.'

'Besides, unlike you, I barely knew my parents. I loved them, of course, but all my life they were like strangers. They were always off somewhere. I scarcely ever saw them.'

As he spoke, Josh picked up one of the silver-framed photographs that were arranged, their backs to Sally, on the little table beside him. No doubt it contained a picture of his parents, Sally decided, as he glanced at it briefly then laid it down again.

He smiled. 'No, Aunt Mimi was my real family. She was more of a mother to me than my own mother ever was.'

His eyes narrowed as he said it and Sally guessed what he was thinking. He was reflecting on how deeply he despised her for having twice betrayed the woman he loved so much. Once with the necklace and now again through the shop. Aunt Mimi had rented it out to her in good faith, and she had employed it as a front for her crimes.

Except that none of that was true. It was Josh who believed it.

She opened her mouth to speak. Suddenly it mattered that he knew the truth. And not just the truth about the counterfeit pottery—that was destined to be revealed to him soon enough—but also the truth about the necklace.

But before she could speak he took her by surprise.

He said, 'You know, I always envied you.'

'Envied *me*?' What a very peculiar notion!

'Yes, envied *you*. Don't look so disbelieving! You had a lot for a boy like me to envy.' His expression was sincere but devoid of self-pity. Self-pity was not an emotion that Josh had ever been prey to.

'Look at what you had,' he continued, watching her, laying his long tanned hands along the brocade arms of his chair. 'You had all the things that are most important—a wonderful close family and two

loving parents who were always there for you when
you needed them.'

Sally could not deny it. She had been blessed and
she knew it. Still, she frowned, out of confusion
more than anything.

'But you had . . . so many other things.'

'Expensive toys and stuff, you mean?'

Sally nodded. 'You had a speedbike that was the
envy of all the other kids. Nobody else had seen
anything like it in the village!'

'Yes, I remember that bike.' A smile flitted across
his eyes. 'I remember riding it off a bridge once
and breaking my arm. My parents never even knew
about that accident. They'd have been furious at
me for almost wrecking the bike!'

He laughed as he said it, but though Sally laughed
back she felt a spurt of hurt and anger on his behalf.
How terrible to have had parents who cared more
about a bicycle than they did about their son's
broken arm.

'So, you see . . .' she continued to watch him as
he went on ' . . . I've always considered you to be
one of the luckiest people I know.'

'I suppose I am.'

She thought again of what he must be thinking—
how badly she'd turned out in spite of all her ad-
vantages—and again she was filled with a pressing
need to tell him the truth about Aunt Mimi's
necklace. For that, she felt certain, was at the root
of everything.

But as she opened her mouth to tell him, she was
silenced as he said, 'I'm astonished that someone
with your background could get involved with
someone like Clive.'

'Clive?'

Sally frowned back at him, feeling oddly jarred at this sudden introduction of Clive into the conversation. It felt totally incongruous. Clive didn't belong in this discussion. This discussion was private, about her and Josh.

And perhaps it was the guilt she felt at her reaction, as well as the suddenly hard look in Josh's eyes, that caused her to tell him sharply, 'Clive's none of your damned business!'

'Thank heavens for that.' His tone was steely. 'Clive is not someone I would wish to be my business.' He fixed her with a look, as cold as an ice-cap. 'And neither, if you had any taste, would you.'

He smiled dismissively. 'Your taste and mine may coincide on frivolous, unimportant matters like décor. But they are unhappily miles apart on more important matters—like who we choose, or do not choose, for our friends.'

In an instant, with that brutal declaration, he had swept away all the warmth and rapport between them. It had meant nothing to him, Sally realised. The cosy chat they'd been having, to him, was just a way of passing the time. She hated him for just how much that hurt her.

She clenched her fists and hissed across at him, 'Oh, but you're wrong, I do care who I choose for my friends. That's why you need never fear that I might choose you!'

And suddenly, once again, she no longer cared whether he knew the truth about the necklace—or any of it, really, come to that. She didn't care what he thought of her. He was vicious and arrogant.

The only thing she cared about was clearing her name.

At that moment the door opened and the butler appeared, pushing a silver trolley before him.

'Your coffee, sir,' he intoned.

Josh nodded and looked at Sally, a look that chilled her to the marrow.

'Let's drink this up quickly and get down to business,' he told her. 'Personally, I can't wait to see what develops.'

Sally was in full agreement with that sentiment. Only she knew what was about to develop. Her name would be cleared.

So why, she wondered, did she feel so nervous as she climbed into the passenger seat of the red Ferrari and watched Josh turn the key in the ignition, making the engine roar to life? There could only be one outcome to this expedition to the craft shop, and that was a cause for rejoicing, not anxiety.

It was just that everything about Josh suddenly put her on edge. One minute he was smiling at her, the next breathing fire—and though she kept telling herself that that was nothing new, that she ought to be used to that by now, she was finding it increasingly hard to cope with.

For she was learning, to her dismay, that he still had the power to hurt her. He still had the power to lay waste her soul. And it seemed there wasn't a thing she could do to protect herself.

But with an effort, at least outwardly, she was keeping control.

She turned to him as he slid the gear lever into first. 'I'd understood that we'd be going on foot. After all, you told me it took twice as long by car... and I thought you hated wasting precious time.'

Josh ignored the sarcasm in her tone. 'Don't worry,' he told her, 'it won't be wasted. I shall enjoy every minute as I sit and watch you desperately trying to concoct some story that will save your hide when we get to the shop.' He tossed her a smile. 'Or have you already thought of one?'

'I don't need a story.'

Sally tried to hold his gaze, but that hard look in his eyes made her look away. And, suddenly, though she knew that what she said was true, she felt the uneasiness inside her growing. He seemed so sure he was going to catch her out. Was it possible that he knew something she didn't?

The journey to the other side of the park in fact took half the time Josh had predicted. In what seemed like no time at all, to Sally's consternation, they were drawing up outside a blue-painted shop with, above the door, the legend 'Prinny's Arts & Crafts'.

'This is it. Are you ready?' Josh turned to look at her.

'Of course I'm ready.' Sally snatched at the door-handle. 'I've never been more ready for anything in my life.' But deep inside, though it should not have been, her heart was quaking.

A moment later they were heading across the pavement to the shop. A bell jangled—a little too merrily for Sally's ears—as Josh pushed the door open and bade her enter ahead of him. This was it, she was thinking. The moment of truth. She just wished she was feeling a little more confident.

A woman was seated behind the counter. Josh approached her, smiling. 'Miss Jamieson, Josh Kingsley. Perhaps you remember me? I've come to see your boss if he's around.'

From the way Miss Jamieson shot, beaming, out of her seat, it was plain she remembered Josh very well indeed. He had obviously made his usual stunning impression!

'Mr Kingsley! How nice to see you!' She thrust a heavily ringed hand at him. 'But Mr Aitken's not here, I'm afraid. He's gone to Bath today.'

Through her tension Sally felt a thrust of disappointment. This was one eventuality she hadn't considered.

She sighed inwardly, sensing sharply that Josh was disappointed, too. He was saying to Miss Jamieson, 'When do you expect him back?'

'Oh, he'll be back late tonight...and he'll be here in the shop tomorrow.' Miss Jamieson smiled solicitously. 'Perhaps I can help you in the meantime?'

Josh had started to turn away, but he paused now, frowning. Then he smiled. 'Who knows? Perhaps you can. It's about those pottery owls...and the girl who sold them to Mr Aitken...' He gestured towards Sally. 'Is this her?'

'This girl here?'

As Miss Jamieson proceeded to examine her, Sally suddenly felt like the solo participant in some police identity parade. It was not a feeling that she cared for in the slightest.

Miss Jamieson peered and peered. 'I never actually spoke to her. I only saw her with Mr Aitken in his office. But I suppose I had a fairly good look at her...'

She peered some more, then turned to Josh, 'Yes,' she said, 'this looks like her.'

'What? What are you saying? It wasn't me!' In horror Sally stepped forward to confront the woman. 'How can you say that? It wasn't me!'

Miss Jamieson drew back, blanching a little. But her alarm had done nothing to change her mind. In fact, as she addressed herself to Josh again, she sounded even more certain than ever.

'Yes, I would definitely say that was her.'

'This is crazy!' Sally started to take another step towards her, but Josh had laid a restraining hand on her arm.

'Thank you, Miss Jamieson,' he said. 'You've been most helpful.' Then, as Sally continued to splutter incoherently, he added, 'Tell Mr Aitken we'll drop in first thing tomorrow morning—just so he can confirm your identification.'

Then, as Miss Jamieson intoned, 'I look forward to seeing you,' he proceeded to steer Sally towards the exit.

'Good afternoon,' he nodded politely, pushing Sally outside.

'That was monstrous! How could she say that? She's never seen me before in her life!' Sally was quivering with emotion as Josh led her towards the car. She flung round to face him. 'Did you set that up or what?'

He regarded her pale face. 'I didn't need to set it up. The woman, quite clearly, was speaking the truth.'

'She was speaking a load of nonsense!' Sally could scarcely stand upright. Her anger and disbelief and confusion and resentment were suddenly pulling her in all directions. She almost felt like weeping. 'The woman's an idiot! She obviously suffers from hallucinations!'

'She doesn't seem like an idiot to me. She seems like a perfectly sane person.' Josh flicked her a look. 'Now get in the car.'

'No, I won't get in the car!' Sally tried to pull away from him. 'You've set this whole thing up! You're trying to frame me! You've always hated me. This is some sick revenge!'

Josh's face had closed against her. 'Don't make a scene,' he warned her. 'Just do as you're told and get in the car.'

'No, I won't do as I'm told, and I won't get in the car!' Sally was oblivious to passers-by glancing in her direction. 'I'm getting out of here! I'm sick of these games of yours! I'm going back to the village and you can't stop me!'

But she was no match for his strength, even in this adrenalin-charged state. Quietly, but firmly, Josh continued to steer her towards the car.

'No, I won't go!'

His hand was on the door-handle. 'Stop it, Sally. Just get in the car and calm down.'

'No, I won't calm down! And I won't get in the car! Damn your car! Damn it and damn you!'

And, suddenly, as though possessed by demons, she was shaking him off and turning on him in fury.

'Why?' she demanded. 'Why do you have to do this to me? Why can't you leave me alone? What have I ever done to you? Why do you hate me? Why? Why? Why?'

Then, gulping for air, all the strength drained out of her, she just stood there and let the tears pour helplessly down her face. Suddenly she wished she could just fall into the gutter and die.

There was a silence that echoed. Then Josh said quietly, 'I think you should get in the car now, Sally.'

His hand was on her arm—but more supportive than controlling. His touch was gentle. He was not pushing her.

Then he tilted her chin and, very gently, stroked away the tears with the flat of his thumb. 'Let's go home,' he said kindly. 'Get in the car.'

Sally had no more resistance. She collapsed into the passenger seat. Then the door was slamming shut and Josh was walking round to climb into the driver's seat beside her.

On the drive back to the apartment not a word was spoken. Sally stared miserably out the window. What was there to say?

Back at the apartment Sally made a tactical withdrawal.

'I'd like a bath, if you don't mind,' she put to Josh, without looking at him, the moment they stepped through the penthouse door.

'I'll get Roberts to show you your room.' Josh had no objections. It would probably be a relief to him to be rid of her for a while.

A moment later, as if by magic, Roberts the butler appeared and proceeded to lead her to a big bright room, all decorated in yellow taffeta and overlooking the park.

'The bathroom's here, miss.' He pushed open a door to reveal a lavish buttercup-tiled bathroom. 'Is there anything else you require?'

'No, thank you.' She shook her head and threw him a smile, responding to the genuinely concerned note in his voice. She had laughed at him before—though not unkindly—but this was no stereotype robot before her. This was a kind-hearted man whose sharp eyes had noticed the mascara-smudged tear-stains on her face. 'I'll be fine,' she assured him. 'A warm bath is all I need.'

Of course it was not all she needed. She realised that. What she needed, and desperately, was for this nightmare to end. But a warm bath helped. As she lay among the bubbles, Sally almost began to feel half human again.

She stared at the buttercup tiles. *Was* she the victim of some conspiracy? Had Josh set this whole thing up, as she had accused him?

Her brain spun round in circles. It didn't make sense. Why would he put himself to so much trouble? Could he really hate her that much?

She swallowed hard and closed her eyes. That was a hard one to bear.

Then she thought about Clive. Had he returned to the village yet? She must phone him, she decided, as soon as she'd had her bath. Perhaps *he* could throw some light on this whole mystery.

But there was no answer at Clive's flat when half an hour later she tried calling from the phone on her bedside table. And Sharon had no news of him when Sally called her at the shop. He just seemed to have vanished. It really was odd.

She sank back on the bed, wrapping the big yellow towel round her, and stared in puzzlement at the ceiling. Tomorrow, if all went well, she'd be meeting Mr Aitken, and he, with any luck, would prove more helpful than his assistant.

But she couldn't count on that. She couldn't count on anything. Two and two, it suddenly seemed, no longer added up to four.

It was when she'd been lying there for a good half-hour, lost in her mental machinations, that suddenly a light tap sounded on the door.

Sally knew instantly that it was Roberts. Josh was incapable of knocking so discreetly! Almost grateful for the interruption, for her brain was growing weary, she arranged the huge bathsheet like a toga, then opened the door a fraction and stuck her head round.

Sure enough, it was Roberts. His kindly face smiled at her. 'Mr Kingsley asks if you would care to join him. He's in the main drawing-room. He has some guests he'd like you to meet.'

'Guests?' Sally blinked. Why would he want her to meet his guests? She would have thought he'd be glad if she just stayed in her room!

Then a thought occurred to her. Maybe these guests of his had something to do with the pottery owls!

She nodded at Roberts. 'I'll be there in five minutes.'

And, sure enough, she was. Her damp hair combed, dressed in a fresh pair of cotton trousers and a simple top the same colour as her eyes, she stepped into the drawing-room, her head held high, a sudden spurt of optimism in her heart.

But she knew instantly that she had been mistaken.

The two women there had nothing to do with pottery owls. Prinny's Arts & Crafts Shop was definitely not their style. They'd be more into Gucci or Chanel!

Sally felt her heart sink as she stepped into the room, wishing she'd been less keen to accept the invitation to join them. But there was no backing out now. Josh was stepping forward to introduce her.

'This is Sally,' he was saying, 'a good friend of mine. Sally and I have known one another for years.'

That last part was true enough. But the 'good friend' bit was outrageous! Sally wondered how he managed to keep his face straight. But Josh was good at these things. Sally stiffened her spine. She would show him that she could be good at them, too!

A moment later, twice, she was clasping manicured fingers and seating herself in one of the brocade-covered armchairs. 'How lovely to meet you,' she was saying, as though she meant it.

'You're a painter, I believe,' one of the women— Jo—was saying. 'What kind of painting do you do?'

'Sort of modern . . . but not abstract. I like doing portraits.' Sally smiled at her. 'I really enjoy painting people.'

'It's the best subject in the world, after all,' Jo
agreed with her. 'What could be more fascinating
than painting people?'

'And she's very good at it, too.'

It was Josh who had spoken. His eyes were on
her and he was smiling with what looked discon-
certingly like pride. He really was an excellent actor!

Sally smiled back at him. 'Thank you,' she told
him. When she tried, she wasn't a bad actress
herself! Then she turned to Jo. 'And what do you
do?'

To Sally's surprise the encounter turned out to
be most enjoyable. Jo and her friend Sunny, Sally
soon discovered, were actually two interesting and
very nice people. In the course of the hour that
followed, the conversation was lively, ranging from
painting to apple strudel and touching on just about
everything in between!

There was just one moment in the proceedings
when Sally found herself thrown, and that had
nothing to do with Jo and Sunny.

Roberts had come into the room with a pot of
fresh coffee, and it was as she'd turned fleetingly
to smile at him that Sally's eye had fallen suddenly
on the silver photo-frame she'd seen Josh look at
earlier.

Her heart had stopped like a stone in her chest.
She'd blinked hard and looked again. But no, she
wasn't seeing things.

It wasn't a photograph of his parents, as Sally
had supposed. It was a picture of Josh and Aunt
Mimi, taken in Aunt Mimi's garden—and with
them, though slightly out of focus and in the background, was Sally, wearing a bright summer dress.

How extraordinary, she thought. Surely he hadn't noticed she was on it!

She'd glanced at Josh, frowning, and was suddenly taken aback as, inexplicably, he'd raised his eyes to hers and winked. Confused, she'd looked away, blushing to her hair roots.

Then, at last, Jo and Sunny were gathering up their things and leaving.

'I hope we'll meet again.' Sunny shook Sally's hand warmly. And Sally smiled, but said nothing. She felt the same way, but she knew they would never see one another again. The masquerade would end as soon as the two girls were out the door.

She drifted back into the drawing-room after the farewells were over. What now? she was wondering, as Josh drifted in behind her. It was only five o'clock. They had the whole evening to kill.

'So, how are you feeling now?'

Sally turned round as Josh spoke to her. He was standing by the walnut bureau, his hands in his pockets. And she couldn't help it—her heart turned over at the sight of him. There was something in his eyes that seemed to reach to her soul.

She said, glancing away from him, trying to shake the feeling from her, 'I'm fine. Why do you ask?' Her heart was racing.

'I thought it might cheer you up to spend an hour with Jo and Sunny. They turned up unexpectedly, while you were having your bath. I thought they'd help to take you out of yourself a bit.'

Sally remembered then. She felt her cheeks colour. She'd entirely forgotten about her outburst earlier.

She smiled a small smile and agreed, 'I think they did.'

'Good. I'm glad to hear it.' He had taken a step towards her. 'I hated to see you so upset.' The dark eyes watched her closely. 'Are you sure you're all right?'

'Yes, thanks, I've recovered.' His concern was disconcerting. Sally shifted uncomfortably, wondering what had prompted it. He didn't have to act now. His two friends were gone.

'Look, let me make a suggestion,' he said now, taking another step towards her. Suddenly, he was standing very close.

Too close, thought Sally, as she looked up at him uneasily. 'What suggestion?' she asked him, her voice a little gruff.

'This...' All at once, his hands were on her arms, as light as gossamer, scorching like hot irons. 'Since we have to spend the rest of the evening together and I really don't want to see you upset again, I suggest we make a truce.'

He took a deep breath. 'Let's not talk about anything even remotely connected with pottery owls.' He smiled. 'What do you say? Do you think it's a good idea?'

It sounded an excellent idea. Sally nodded, watching him. Pottery owls were the last things she wanted to think about. For, suddenly, what filled her mind was the way he was looking at her, the long-lashed dark eyes all at once soft and melting. She loved the way those melting dark eyes made her feel.

She smiled a little foolishly. 'OK,' she agreed. 'We definitely won't say a word about owls.'

'Promise?'

'I promise.'

'Good. So, that's settled, then.'

But he did not move away, and he did not release her.

And Sally did not want him to. She continued to gaze up at him, her heart tapping inside her like the wind at a temple door.

And it felt like forever before he finally bent to kiss her.

CHAPTER SEVEN

IT HAD to be a dream. Josh kissing her? Surely not!

But, dream or not, it felt amazing. Sally sank against him, surrendering happily to the blissful sensations that suddenly poured through her. It was as though she'd been waiting for this kiss all her life.

His arms held her softly, pressing her against him. She could feel the warmth and the strength of him invade her, making her heart knock like a fist against her ribcage. And as his hands gently caressed her she could feel tingles down her spine, darting up to her scalp and down to the soles of her feet. She loved the feel of those strong, sure hands.

But it was the touch of his lips that really galvanised her. Their heat burned, sending hot and cold shivers through her, causing her blood to leap with excitement and pound like some raging torrent through her veins.

For there was a fire in his lips that filled her with sudden yearning, with dreams and desires she had never known before. It was as though, without warning, she had suddenly been catapulted into a realm of the senses of whose existence she'd been unaware. It felt strange and unreal and dangerous and exciting. She longed to step beyond the threshold and explore.

As his lips pressed hers, teasing her, ever-gentle, she was filled with the sweet, intoxicating taste of him. Her lips parted in welcome, greedy for him, eager for him. His kisses were like wine. They filled her to the brim.

But, too swiftly, it was all over. He was stepping away from her, although his arms still embraced her, circling her waist.

He looked down into her face. 'That was nice. I enjoyed that.' His dark eyes darted with warm, gentle humour. 'I reckon we ought to have done that sooner.'

Sally flushed to her hair roots. What had she been thinking of? She had allowed herself to be swept away by his kisses, and to him all they had been was a pleasant diversion!

She slipped from his embrace, impatient with herself. What else had she expected? She was the one who was mad!

'I suppose it was quite nice, but it shouldn't have happened.' She looked at him as levelly as she was able, considering the still frantic state of her heart. 'I'm afraid you caught me unawares.'

Josh's smile simply widened. He raised one dark eyebrow. 'Then I must try to catch you unawares more often.'

'No, I don't think you should try that.'

'No?'

As he continued to smile at her, Sally felt almost painfully vulnerable, suddenly totally, hopelessly undermined by the stupefying power of the emotions that gripped her.

It was a familiar sensation—or, at least, it had been, once. Once, when she had known no better, when she had been an innocent child.

That thought sent a surge of resistance through her. She cast her childish, undermining emotions from her. They had no place in her heart any more.

She repeated, a little more firmly, a little more convincingly than the first time, 'No, I definitely don't think you should try that again.'

'Pity.' He continued to smile at her wickedly. 'I could really get to like it.'

'Well, I couldn't.' She stepped away from him, hoping the lie sounded convincing. 'In fact, I found it quite distasteful.'

'Distasteful?' He let his dark eyes skip over her lightly, evidently amused by her outrageously false claim. 'I would never have guessed it. In fact, I would have said the opposite.'

And how right he was—but what a nerve he had to say it! Sally thinned her lips at him disapprovingly. 'Then you deceive yourself,' she told him tightly. 'Not all women, as you seem to believe, happen to find you irresistible.'

'Is that what I believe?'

'Do you actually deny it?' She threw the challenge at him with unconcealed irritation—though the irritation she felt was with herself as much as him. Why was she pursuing this dangerously loaded conversation? Why didn't she simply put an end to it?

But she didn't. Instead, she added, 'You've always believed it. You've always believed no woman could resist you.'

'No woman except you, that is. You've always resisted me.'

'Resist you? Oh, no, I've never had to resist you. Resistance is only necessary when there is temptation in the first place.' Sally smiled with satisfaction as she continued with this pleasing argument, 'I'm terribly sorry to dent your ego, but although every other woman on the planet may have been tempted, this one, fortunately, never has been.'

Josh laughed at that and shook his head, his ego apparently quite undented. 'Well said,' he acknowledged, eyeing her with mischief. 'That, if I may say so, was typical Sally.' Then, as she frowned, wondering precisely what he'd meant by that, he elaborated, 'I've always admired that independent streak of yours. You like to think for yourself, go your own way. Not many people do. It says a lot for you.'

Sally blushed—to her utter, unendurable mortification. Surprise, she told herself, at this unexpected praise. For praise of her more personal qualities was not something Josh went in for. Total condemnation was more what she was used to hearing.

But, though her cheeks betrayed her surprise, she said nothing. She simply looked back at him as steadily as she was able and tried to tell him with her eyes that, deep down, she was unmoved. She had not taken the false compliment to heart.

For it was false. She knew that, even without thinking about it. Josh was incapable of feeling anything positive towards her.

Josh glanced suddenly at his watch. 'On that note,' he was saying, 'I suggest we retire to our separate rooms and start getting ready for dinner.' He slipped his hands into his trouser pockets and glanced down at her, eyebrows lifted. 'I suggest we dine early. About seven o'clock. Can you be ready in an hour or so's time?'

What was he planning? Dinner *à deux* at some fancy London restaurant? Sally stepped away from him. She wanted no part of that. She said, 'I think I'd rather just have a bite to eat here.'

'It's Roberts' evening off.'

'I can cook for myself. I don't need anything fancy. An omelette would do.'

'No, an omelette wouldn't do. It's been a long time since lunchtime.' He started to turn away. 'Try to be ready by six-thirty.'

'I'd really rather not. *You* go to a restaurant.' She fixed the back of his neck with her eyes. 'You really don't have to feel obliged to take me with you. I'm perfectly capable of feeding myself.'

'That independent spirit of yours rising to the surface again?' Josh paused to smile knowingly at her over his shoulder. Then he narrowed his dark eyes at her in a look that brooked no argument. 'You're my guest. You'll come with me. Kindly be ready in an hour.'

Sally could easily have been ready in half that time. Was he expecting her to appear all coiffed and perfumed, done up to the nines like one of his girlfriends? she wondered, as she gave her hair a vigorous brushing. Had he forgotten she was already wearing her only modest change of clothes?

She glared at her reflection irritably. Why was he inflicting this on them? For he must dislike the thought of dinner together every bit as much as she did. He was only insisting on it, she suspected, because she had tried to resist him. Josh had never had much of a taste for being opposed.

Sally was waiting for him in the drawing-room when he appeared, dressed in a casual jacket and trousers and open-necked shirt. At least there was one thing to be grateful for, Sally reflected—he wasn't planning to show her up by taking her somewhere like the Ritz!

'Are you ready? Let's go, then.' He stood watching her in the doorway. 'Or would you like a drink before we leave?'

'Not particularly.' Pointedly, Sally rose to her feet. The sooner it got started, the sooner the evening would be over. She had no desire to spin it out.

'Good. We can have an aperitif there.' Josh was leading her across the hallway towards the front door. Then they were taking the lift down to the ground floor and heading down the stone steps on to the street.

The Ferrari was parked there, but, 'We'll walk,' Josh told her. 'I want to be able to have a glass or two of wine.' He paused. 'Unless, of course, you want to do the driving?'

Some hope! With a wry smile Sally slanted a glance at the mean-looking red machine at the kerbside. The thought of sitting behind the wheel of that in the midst of chaotic London traffic was enough to bring her out in goosebumps!

She flicked Josh a smile. 'No, thanks,' she declined, knowing his offer had only been a joke anyway. 'I, too, would prefer a couple of glasses of wine.'

In the event they each had several glasses of wine. Josh chose a light red that proved a perfect accompaniment to their tortellini followed by veal. For he had taken her to a jolly little Italian trattoria, just fifteen minutes' walk from the flat, and the sort of informal little place that Sally loved. She was rather glad she hadn't settled for an omelette in the kitchen!

And even Josh's company, as it turned out, proved quite agreeable. At least for the first part of the evening.

He started off by reminding her, 'We agreed on a truce, remember? So, if you'll stop scowling at me, I promise I won't scowl at you.'

Had she been scowling? Sally blinked, faintly thrown. The truth was, she'd been reflecting, as he poured them both some wine, that being with him like this felt quite astonishingly natural. As natural as that kiss whose memory still lingered.

She crushed the thought instantly. That kiss had been a mistake, just as this temporary truce was an illusion. Nothing had changed between them. They were still sworn enemies.

Still, she nodded and responded, smiling, 'OK, I'll stop scowling.' She raised her wine glass in a toast. 'Here's to our truce.'

The evening proceeded in light-hearted vein, with Josh regaling Sally with amusing stories about his various adventures all over the world.

'Don't you ever lose track of yourself?' Sally put to him, joking. 'If I were moving around the globe at the rate you do, I think I'd end up totally bewildered.'

'No, you wouldn't.' He eyed her. 'You'd enjoy it. I'm sure it would provide you with inspiration for your painting.'

'Perhaps,' she conceded, lowering her eyes briefly. She'd always wished she could afford to see more of the world and had hoped the shop might bring in the necessary extra money. Now, of course, she could put all such foolish hopes behind her. She'd be lucky if she could manage to pay her grocery bills now, never mind indulge in foreign holidays!

But she did not say that. That would only have soured the atmosphere. She said instead, 'Anyway, it seems to inspire you. No one could complain about the way your business is going.'

'No, I suppose not.'

'I would say definitely not.' Sally glanced across at him with genuine admiration. Not many people achieved what Josh had achieved—including a flat in Regent's Park and a shiny red Ferrari! Then she found herself adding, without a shadow of irony, 'I always knew you'd do well. I've never doubted it for a minute.'

'Such faith.'

'Why not?' She smiled as she said it, and Josh was smiling, too, warm amusement in his eyes. Then she couldn't resist it. She remembered his claim and teased him, 'Maybe you're not the only one who's a good judge of character.'

Josh laughed then, making Sally laugh, and as their eyes met and held it felt oddly exhilarating, as well as perfectly natural that they should suddenly be so easy in one another's company. It made Sally wonder, fleetingly, if maybe they hadn't always been and it was just she who had imagined all the disharmony.

But she was too focused on the present to pause to consider that. As his eyes twinkled across at her, she added, 'After all, I had many years in which to observe you.'

'So that's what you were really up to when you were sitting in a corner, pretending to be scribbling away in your sketching book?' He pulled an amused face. 'You were keeping a beady eye on me?'

'I observed you, yes.' Sally sat back in her seat and tilted her blonde head to one side. 'And, as I said, I always knew you'd go far.'

'You must have found that comforting.' Now he was teasing her. 'I imagine the further you thought I'd go, the happier you must have been.'

Sally almost denied it. It was so far from the truth. There'd been a time when she thought she'd die if she never saw Josh again.

But she kept that to herself and said instead, 'I suppose it's in your blood, a legacy from your parents—this desire to be constantly on the move.'

As soon as she'd said it, Sally regretted the way she'd worded it. A look seemed to flicker at the back of his eyes. But then he smiled. 'You could be right. I do enjoy travelling. But I'm always glad when I get back to London. It's a wonderful city. I often wish I spent more time here.'

That surprised Sally a little. She threw him a teasing look. 'That sounds suspiciously as if you want to put down roots. I always thought you were the original rolling stone.'

'Did you? Well, maybe I used to be.' He smiled and winked at her. 'Maybe I'm mellowing in my old age.'

Sally giggled. 'Definitely not. You show absolutely no signs of that. Thank heavens,' she added, surprising herself and blushing.

Josh half smiled and held her eyes for a moment. And the way he was looking at her made her blood jump. All at once Sally's heart broke into a gallop. She could feel the hairs prickling on the back of her neck.

She turned away abruptly, suddenly covered in confusion, and made a pretence at glancing round the busy trattoria. 'This is a super place. I really like it.'

'Yes, so do I. It's a favourite of mine.' His eyes were still on her, scorching her like lasers. 'When I'm in London I come here all the time.'

'Yes, I guessed that.' She tried to look at him. But it was too unsettling. Her eyes darted away again. 'All the waiters obviously know you.'

And suddenly, as she said it, a new thought occurred to her. Had he brought Karin here? More than likely, she decided. And that thought, which instantly chilled her, led to another, even more chilling. Was Karin the reason for his sudden desire to settle down?

Sally shook herself inwardly. Stop it, she told herself. It doesn't matter to me what Josh and Karin get up to.

Josh had laid down his cutlery and was glancing across at her. 'So tell me about your painting,' he was saying. 'What are you working on at the moment?'

Sally pulled herself together, glad of the change of subject. 'I'm working on a portrait of my mother. I'm doing it mainly from photographs, though she did a couple of sittings for me in the early stages.'

'And are you pleased with it?'

She nodded. 'Pretty pleased. I've been trying out some new techniques and they seem to be working.'

'Are you going to sell it or keep it when you've finished?' Josh picked up his glass and took a mouthful of wine.

Sally hesitated for an instant, considering her answer. Then, suddenly, like a cold hand laid on her heart, she found herself thinking of Karin again.

In a tone that could only be described as hostile, she told him, 'I'll probably sell it, if I can find a buyer. A struggling artist can't afford to be sentimental...especially,' she added, looking him straight in the eye, 'when her alternative means of support has somewhat unexpectedly been snatched from her.'

Damn his stupid truce! she was suddenly thinking. He's the one to blame for all my problems!

Josh's only reaction was to regard her steadily. 'But surely that's what you really want, anyway— to make a full-time career out of your painting?'

Full marks for cool. He really was amazing. Not a flicker had crossed those unblinking black eyes. Sally was unsure whether to feel admiration or anger. She answered expressionlessly, 'Yes, I suppose it is.'

'It's always been your ambition—at least, that's what I understood. And it would be a waste, in my opinion, for you to do anything else.'

'You mean you've done me a favour by depriving me of my shop?' She had stifled her admiration relatively easily. Pure anger shone from her sea-green eyes. 'Perhaps you think I ought to be grateful?'

'Perhaps you ought to be.' He dared to smile at her. 'Perhaps in years to come you will be.'

There was no answer to that. His gall was colossal. It was an outrageous, unfeeling, cruel thing to say.

He compounded it by adding, 'I was always surprised that you chose to open up a shop in the first place.'

'Were you? I thought you told me you considered it admirable.' She lanced a disapproving look across at him. He'd obviously forgotten that he'd told her that. She held his eyes. 'Or was that a lie?'

Josh sat back in his seat. 'No, it wasn't a lie. I did find it admirable, but I also found it rather surprising. It was the sort of cautious move I'd expect of someone else.' He smiled. 'I thought the Sally I knew was bolder.'

Sally was silenced for a moment. Yes, it had been a cautious move. She'd been aware of that when she'd made it. But she'd had her reasons. She regarded Josh narrowly. 'I wasn't ready to set up as a full-time artist when I left art school. I was still finding my way... stylistically... creatively. I knew I needed a little more time...'

He was watching her, apparently listening. Sally continued, though she suspected he wasn't really interested, 'Besides, I felt the shop could be a useful outlet for my own paintings when I eventually had some to sell. Maybe, eventually, I would have turned it over entirely to my own work.'

'With Clive doing the selling?'

'Yes, that was the idea.' Sally felt oddly wrong-footed at the way he had so casually brought Clive into the conversation. Was it guilt? she wondered fleetingly. Clive had been miles from her thoughts.

Perhaps to expunge her guilt and get back to reality—this evening, until now, had been a travesty of reality—she continued, 'The idea was that eventually I would withdraw from the shop and devote myself exclusively to painting, and Clive would run the shop on his own.'

'I see. A neat idea.' Josh nodded his head. Then he regarded her across the table for a long moment. 'But I'm sure you don't need Clive to sell your paintings for you. I'm sure you can make it on your own.'

Sally purposely did not answer. Was he trying to salve his conscience by talking himself into believing he was really doing her no harm?

Though why should he do that? He *wanted* to do her harm. He believed her a cheat and a thief and a liar.

She felt a coldness go through her, and an unexpected dart of pain. The thought was like ice-water thrown in her face.

Stifling the feeling, she reached for her anger. 'Whether or not I make it will be no thanks to you. So, if you don't mind, I'd really rather not discuss

it. You're not interested anyway, and that suits me
perfectly.'

It was at that moment that the waiter came to
clear away their plates. Heart thumping, Sally sat
back in her chair, grateful for the interruption. This
sudden abrupt shift back to harsh reality had dis-
tressed her far more deeply than it ought to have.

'Do you want a dessert?' Josh was speaking to
her, calmly, apparently unmoved by her little outburst. And why should he be moved? She'd been
right. He didn't care.

Sally shook her head. 'No, thanks. I won't
bother.'

'I don't think I will either. How about coffee?'

Again she shook her head, controlling her
breathing. Suddenly, all she wanted was to be gone
from the restaurant, free of Josh, on her own to
get her head straight.

With relief she heard him say, 'Just bring the bill,
please.' From the corner of her eye she saw him
reach for his wallet. For once, he was actually doing
as she wished. She breathed a huge silent sigh of
relief.

The walk back to the flat was made in virtual
silence, and they walked as far apart from one
another as possible. The façade had been dropped.
Once more, quite openly, they were enemies.

Once up in the penthouse, Josh turned to her
briefly. 'Would you like a nightcap before you go
to bed?' But his tone was steely and she could see
in his eyes that he had no wish for her to take up
his offer. He was as keen to end the evening
as she was.

Sally shook her head obligingly. 'No, I'll go straight to bed.' Then she added politely, 'Thanks for the dinner.'

'Don't mention it. Sleep well.' He turned to take his leave of her. 'I'll see you in the morning. We have business, remember?'

'Oh, I hadn't forgotten.' She met his gaze briefly, lest he think for one moment she was the least bit afraid of their impending meeting with the owner of the craft shop. 'Don't worry, I'll be up bright and early.'

Then, as he moved towards the drawing-room, she turned on her heel and headed swiftly for her room.

And she was not afraid of that meeting tomorrow, Sally told herself, as she got undressed and prepared for bed. Nervous, yes. This whole business made her nervous, but she had no reason to be afraid.

She climbed between the sheets and stared at the ceiling. On the contrary, she had every reason to look forward to tomorrow. Surely this meeting with Mr Aitken would finally clear her name?

Sally tried to focus on that thought as she switched out the light, urging herself to feel calm and cool and positive. She had every reason to feel that way and no reason not to.

Yet, as she stared into the darkness, her heart was heavy, her brain suddenly swarming with confusion. How could she be positive? Maybe Josh had set her up. Maybe tomorrow, when they walked into the craft shop, Mr Aitken would react the same way his assistant had. Sally curled up tight and shivered beneath the bedclothes. Maybe she had every reason to be afraid.

But these weren't the only thoughts that were crowding through her head.

Somehow, through it all, she kept remembering the evening—their brief happy truce and how good it had felt, and that moment in the drawing-room when Josh had kissed her.

And again she melted, her stomach tightening within her. The memory filled her with warmth and despair.

For, even though she knew that those kisses and that truce had meant absolutely nothing to Josh, it would be too cruel to discover that he really had set her up, that he really did hate her as much as that.

Tears slid from her eyes as she pressed her face into the pillow. 'I don't care!' she kept telling herself.

But she did.

Sally had breakfast alone the following morning in the sunny little breakfast-room overlooking a flower-strewn terrace. Josh, so Roberts told her, had eaten some time ago.

No doubt he's desperate to drag me off to the craft shop as soon as possible, she decided a little nervously, spreading a slice of toast with honey. No doubt he's dying to see Mr Aitken point the finger at me. Which he won't, of course, unless he's been paid to.

It was at that moment that Josh appeared in the doorway. 'Will you be ready to leave in half an hour?'

She felt her heart judder as she looked into his face. A sudden swift dart of pain tore through her.

She said, swallowing her toast, shaking the feeling from her, 'Yes, I can be ready whenever you want.'

'OK. Half an hour.' He started to withdraw. 'I'll leave you to finish your breakfast in peace.'

He was still behaving in that polite but oddly distant manner when they met up in the hallway half an hour later. 'Let's go,' he said simply. 'The car's waiting downstairs.'

Sally glanced up at him as he seated himself next to her in the Ferrari. This strange behaviour of his was making her even more nervous. Perhaps he really did have something cooked up, after all.

They made the journey to the shop in a matter of minutes. Too quickly, Sally thought with a snatch of anxiety, as they parked outside the blue-painted façade. Then they were climbing out of the car and walking across the pavement, Josh in front, Sally behind. Suddenly her stomach was tied up in knots.

Miss Jamieson opened the door for them.

'Good morning, Mr Kingsley,' she murmured, ushering them inside. Then she added, 'Come with me. Mr Aitken's waiting.' A moment later she was leading them to the office at the back of the shop.

Suddenly Sally's anxiety was growing again. It peaked as the woman murmured, 'Please go in.' And Sally's heart stood still as the door was pushed open and suddenly, on stiff legs, she was stepping inside.

There was one thing for sure, she told herself nervously, as the figure behind the desk began to rise to his feet. She had never set eyes on him before. But what mattered, of course, was what *he* had to say. Her heart was thundering as he peered into her face.

It seemed like forever before he finally spoke. But then, slowly detaching his eyes from Sally's face, he addressed himself directly to Josh.

'No, this isn't the girl,' he said quite simply.

Sally let out a gasp. She turned to Josh. But Josh's eyes were on Aitken. 'Are you absolutely sure?'

'Couldn't be surer.' Mr Aitken nodded firmly. 'The hair's the same and so's the height and the general build. But this isn't the girl. She's a different type altogether.' He paused and turned to smile at Sally. 'For one thing, this young lady is a great deal prettier.'

Sally was grinning. She couldn't help it. Finally, she was cleared of all the crimes of which Josh had accused her. That was the best feeling in the world. A huge weight off her shoulders. She felt like leaping across the desk and hugging Mr Aitken.

And there was another thing, too, that made her heart glow. She looked across at Josh, silly relief flooding through her. He hadn't framed her, after all. He hadn't set her up. He might still hate her, but he didn't hate her that much!

'I owe you an apology.'

They were back in the car. Ten minutes had passed, they'd taken their leave of Mr Aitken and now, Sally assumed, they were headed back to the flat.

But Josh was turning to face her as he switched on the engine. He said again, 'I owe you an apology. How can you ever forgive me for this?'

'I don't know.' It was the truth. She looked into his face and absorbed the sincerity that flowed from his eyes. But there was something else there too, something that baffled her. She observed, narrowing her eyes at him, 'You're taking this all very calmly. You scarcely batted an eyelid back there in Mr Aitken's office.'

It was true. His expression, throughout the brief interview, hadn't altered by a single thread. It had remained as calm and reticent and reserved as it had been when she had first set eyes on him this morning. He looked at her now and revealed the reason why.

In a flat tone he told her, 'I already knew.'

'Knew what?'

'That it wasn't you.'

Sally felt her mouth drop open. 'What do you mean you knew it wasn't me? Are you trying to tell me you knew all along?'

'Not all along, no. I wish I had. But I've known since eight o'clock this morning.' He frowned. 'I was going to suggest that we call off the meeting with Aitken, but then I decided it was probably best that we go through with it—just in order to make absolutely sure.'

'To make sure about what?' Sally had turned towards him. What was going on? He was speaking in riddles.

'To make sure that my information was correct—though I have to say that I was pretty sure it was.'

Sally was none the wiser. She leaned towards him. 'Would you mind telling me what you're talking about?'

'You're not going to like it.'

She already had that feeling. There was something about the strangely reserved look in his eyes that had already caused her heart to clench.

In a firm tone she told him, 'I haven't liked any of it much so far...so you really needn't be so worried about telling me. I'm beginning to get used to receiving nasty shocks.'

But still he hesitated. 'This one concerns Clive.' He held her eyes. 'Clive and another girl.'

She had not expected that. Sally withdrew a little. 'Clive and another girl? What do you mean another girl?'

'*The* other girl is perhaps what I should say.' Josh took a deep breath. 'The one that Aitken met. The one who passed herself off as you.' He sighed. 'I have information as to where she and Clive might be. If you like, we can go and check it out—or we can simply leave the whole thing to the police.'

Sally was struggling to understand. Her heart was racing. She heard herself say, 'Where are they supposed to be?'

'Highgate. Not far.' He paused. 'It's up to you. If you want, we can go... The decision is yours.'

It was the sympathy in his eyes that caused her to turn away. He felt sorry for her, and that was almost as hard to bear as hate.

'OK.' Her voice was firm, though her heart was barely beating. She had said she had grown used to receiving nasty shocks, but she wasn't quite sure if she was ready for this one. She forced herself to add, 'Let's go now. Right away.'

'Are you sure?'

'I'm sure.'

She had no chance to change her mind. The next instant they were surging away from the kerbside, heading for north London and the truth at last.

CHAPTER EIGHT

'IF YOU'RE having second thoughts, we can always turn back now.' Josh spoke suddenly as he negotiated the traffic. 'It's not too late and I would quite understand.'

They had just whizzed past a signpost declaring 'Highgate ½ mile', and Sally's stomach was a solid lump of stone inside her. It was tempting to say, OK. Let's just leave it to the police, but she forced herself to shake her head.

In a firm tone, she answered, 'No, I want to go. I want to find out face to face exactly what's going on. I've been an ignorant bystander in all this for far too long.'

She was aware that, as she spoke, her voice was shaky, and she sensed Josh's sympathetic glance in her direction. But she did not look back at him. She could not have borne to meet his eyes. Right now she could not have borne to meet the eyes of anyone—but particularly not the bright, sharp eyes of Josh.

Inside, she felt quite numb as she struggled to come to grips with the shocking truth that was gradually starting to dawn on her. And the distress she felt, she knew, was shining from her eyes. Her expression, she sensed, was fearful and ragged. She had no wish to expose her emotional nakedness to Josh.

'This is it.'

Suddenly they were turning into a leafy sub-
urban street and Josh was slowing the car and
peering at house numbers. Then he nodded as he
drew up alongside the kerb. 'It's that one with the
green door and the grey Volvo outside.'

The car was Clive's. Sally had recognised it instantly. Her heart had twisted inside her at the sight
of it.

'Yes,' she said, forcing herself to sound calm.
'And it looks as though he's in.'

She reached for the door-handle. 'Will you wait
here?' she asked Josh. 'I don't know how long I'll
be. I expect not too long.'

But Josh was opening his own door. 'I'm coming
with you. I won't allow you to go in there alone.'

Sally spun round to face him then. 'Oh, but I
must go in alone! This is private. Between Clive
and me. I don't want you to come with me!'

Josh shook his head. 'I think I ought to. I'm not
sure you can handle this on your own.'

Sally wasn't sure either, but she knew she had to.
She took a deep breath. 'I can handle it. Don't
worry.' Then she smiled a wry smile. 'Have no fear,
he's not dangerous. At least not in any physical
sense.'

Josh smiled back at her, a gentle, sympathetic
smile that made Sally instantly snatch her eyes away.
She could not bear for him to look at her in that
fashion. It unravelled her sense of purpose. It
twisted her up inside. She could scarcely breathe
for the lump it had brought to her throat.

She turned away abruptly and stared blindly
through the windscreen. 'Please,' she said softly.

'Give me a few minutes alone with him. Then you can come in if you wish.'

'OK. You've got ten minutes.' Josh made the concession grudgingly. He dropped his hand from the door-handle and sat back in his seat. 'Ten minutes, remember. That's all,' he repeated.

Sally nodded a brief acknowledgement and began to slide from the car, her bag clutched in her hand as though it were a shield. Then on stiff legs she was striding towards the green door, praying for the strength to hold on to her composure in the face of whatever was destined to happen next. Just don't let me make a fool of myself. That's all I ask.

She pressed the doorbell and heard chimes in the hall. Then she was forcing herself to breathe calmly and deeply at the sound of footsteps heading towards her.

A moment later the door opened and she found herself looking into the face of a blonde-haired, blue-eyed girl.

So this is my impersonator, she found herself thinking in an oddly detached fashion that surprised her a little. She had expected to feel a little more emotion.

The girl was staring at her. 'Yes?' she demanded in an aggressive tone. Then she added, 'If you're selling something, I'm sorry but I'm not interested.'

'I'm not selling anything.' Suddenly Sally's composure was perfect. She relaxed her tight hold on her bag. 'I've come to see Clive,' she said. 'May I come in?'

'I suppose so.' The girl stood back a little and then, belatedly, she hesitated. 'Who are you? How do I know if Clive wants to see you?'

But as she sought to block her passage Sally was halfway through the door. 'Oh, I shouldn't think he wants to see me,' she told the girl calmly. 'But I intend to see him, anyway. My name's Sally Woodstock.'

The effect of that announcement was deeply pleasing. The blonde girl turned the colour of putty. She shifted uncomfortably. 'Sally Woodstock?' she burbled.

'Yes, the *real* Sally Woodstock.' Sally smiled with grim triumph as, taking advantage of the girl's confusion, she completed her entrance into the hall. 'Now tell me where Clive is.' She glanced around her. 'I want to speak to him and I haven't got much time.'

'He's in the kitchen.' The blonde girl pointed to a half-closed door. But at that moment the door swung open and, beaming broadly, Clive appeared.

'Now this is a surprise!' He stepped towards Sally as though he was genuinely pleased to see her. 'How did you know I was staying with my cousin?'

Sally frowned into his face, feeling a surge of betrayal and dislike, and wondering in amazement at her own unshakeable calmness. She had expected that coming face to face with him would prove more traumatic. But all she was suddenly thinking was that he was a shameless trickster and that she had been an idiot not to see it before.

She looked right through his smile. 'Your cousin, is she? Well, I'm afraid your cousin, like you, has a lot to answer for.'

Clive kept on smiling, but the light in his eyes had faded. 'What are you talking about? Come in and have a cup of tea.'

'To hell with your tea. I'm here on serious business...' As Sally paused, ordering her thoughts before the main onslaught, from behind her the girl's voice cut in.

'I think she knows, Clive.'

'Knows? Knows what?' Still he was bluffing, and now it was Sally's turn to cut in.

'Yes, your girlfriend's right—sorry, your cousin,' she amended sarcastically. 'I know all about what you've been up to. How you used your association with me to cheat a local potter... selling her work in London under a false name and dishonestly pocketing the profits!' She glared at him. 'How could you, Clive? I trusted you!'

'I don't know what you're on about.' His expression was injured innocence. What an actor he was! No wonder she'd been taken in by him. His deceit and her own folly cut her to the marrow.

'Liar!' She stepped towards him, her hands bunched into fists. 'And not only did you cheat the craftspeople we dealt with—for I'll bet Karin Stokes wasn't your only victim—you had the nerve to discredit my name in the process!'

She cast a quick glance behind her at the blonde girl who still stood listening. 'What were you hoping—that, if you were found out, the blame for everything would fall on me? You're scum, Clive! Heaven knows why I didn't spot it sooner!'

'Scum, am I?' Suddenly Clive's demeanour had altered. The false smile had vanished. His lips curled nastily. Thrusting his face at Sally, suddenly he shot back at her, 'You may think I'm scum, but I'm a better businessman than you are. You haven't a clue how to make a profit! Did you seriously think all

I wanted out of life was to run some two-bit craft shop out in the sticks?' He laughed a harsh laugh. 'You must be out of your mind. I used you, you poor fool, right from the start!'

For the first time since she had stepped into the narrow hallway, suddenly Sally's composure was shaken.

She felt herself pale. What he was saying was atrocious—though, surely, she reminded herself through the fog in her head, she had known before she came here that that was the case, that Clive had cynically used her right from the start. But to hear it coming from his own lips was shocking.

She was aware of a bell ringing as she answered shakily, 'Well, your little game's over now. I'm going to see to that.'

'Are you?' Again the bell rang, this time more insistently, though Clive seemed quite oblivious of it as he proceeded to challenge her, 'I don't think you'll find that as easy as you believe. I have all sorts of little operations going on. You may be able to stop a couple of them, but you won't stop me!'

Smiling maliciously, suddenly he was stepping towards her, poking a hard, bony finger in her chest. 'So why don't you just go back to your little village where you belong and get on with scraping a living out of your silly little craft shop and painting pathetic little pictures that'll never sell?'

His finger jabbed and poked, sending her staggering backwards. 'Go on!' he commanded. 'Get out of here!'

Sally wanted to swipe his hand away, but she was about to lose her balance as suddenly her heel caught on the hall rug. She staggered again. Blast!

she was thinking. I'm going to end up in an ignominious heap on the floor!

But that was not to be her fate. Rather more fittingly, it was to be Clive's.

All at once a steadying hand was at her waist and Sally felt a rush of air go past her ear as Josh's fist suddenly shot across her shoulder and made firm, resounding contact with Clive's jaw.

'Get your hands off her!' she heard Josh demand. 'If you want to pick on someone, try picking on me!'

But Clive was in no position to pick on anyone. His eyes widened in surprise as he stumbled backwards and landed with a resounding thump on the floor. He sprawled there, winded, for a moment, then rising slowly he demanded, 'And who the hell are you?'

'I'm your worst nightmares come true, that's who I am.' Josh had stepped in front of Sally to confront him. 'I'm the one who's going to see to it that you *are* stopped—completely! And it's not going to be as hard as you seem to imagine!'

He glared at the other man, who had dropped his eyes away, unable to take the force of that ferocious dark gaze. 'The police are already on to you. They have all your details. So there's no point in you trying to make a run for it. If I were you, I'd just give myself up gracefully.

'And now let's get out of here.' Josh turned to Sally, took her by the arm and propelled her towards the door, past Clive's blonde-haired accomplice who stood stock-still in astonishment, her eyes wide, mutely taking in the scene. 'This place disgusts me. I need some fresh air.'

Gratefully, Sally allowed herself to be steered down the path, out through the gate and down the pavement to the car. Suddenly, uncontrollably, her limbs were shaking. She suspected she would never have made it on her own.

Then she was being bundled into the Ferrari and Josh was climbing in beside her, then reaching across her to fasten her seatbelt.

She felt like a child. Shocked and helpless, stripped of the power of speech and movement, unable to do a single thing for herself. It was as though the enormity of everything that had just happened was only gradually beginning to sink in and the only way she could cope with it was to shut herself in. To remain still and tight and silent and motionless. Barely breathing. Numb to her soul.

Josh seemed to understand. He drove in silence all the way from Highgate to Regent's Park. And his silence was soothing. It was just what she needed. In a funny way it made her feel less alone.

Once outside the flat, he helped her from the car, then led her with a light hand across the hallway and into the lift that took them up to the penthouse. It was only once they were inside the flat that he spoke.

'Sit down,' he told her. 'I'll fix you a drink.'

Sally sat on the edge of one of the brocade-covered sofas. She felt like a piano wire, stretched so tight it might snap. And, if she snapped, she feared the deluge that would follow. Once she snapped she would have no more control of herself.

Josh brought her a drink. 'Brandy,' he told her, helping her boneless fingers to curl around the glass. 'Drink it slowly. It'll make you feel better.'

Nothing could do that. Sally thought it, but did
not say it. Instead, she sipped obediently, then
stared down into the glass. Nothing could erase this
feeling of dazed wretchedness.

Josh had seated himself in an armchair opposite
her and was leaning towards her, a look of concern
on his face. 'Don't take it so hard. He's really not
worth it. Just be glad we all finally know the truth.'

That was easy for him to say. Sally glanced up
at him, swallowing, and forced herself to speak,
though her voice was croaky. 'I believed in him,'
she said. 'I trusted him totally. And right from the
start all he did was use me.'

A look of pain crossed Josh's face. He laid down
his brandy glass. 'I know it must be hard to be faced
with such a thing—especially when you were close
emotionally to the person concerned. But don't
blame yourself for being taken in. The man's a pro-
fessional trickster. He's taken in a lot of people.
He's very good at it. It's what he does for a living.'

'And you warned me, didn't you?' Sally continued to look at him, her features stiff with suppressed emotion. 'You warned me that he'd been
in trouble. And I didn't believe you. I wouldn't
listen.'

'I think that's understandable in the circumstances.' Josh surveyed her face with a tolerant eye.
'One never wants to believe bad of the person one
loves.'

The person one loves? Sally frowned inwardly. I
never loved him, she thought. At least there's that
to be grateful for. But it seemed superfluous to
make the observation out loud. It didn't matter one
way or the other to Josh.

She said instead, feeling knives inside her, struggling to hold back the tears that pricked her eyes, 'And to think that all the time he was despising me and making use of me. How could I have been such a fool?'

'You're no fool, believe me. You trusted him and he betrayed you. That makes him a bastard, but it doesn't make you a fool.' Josh narrowed his eyes at her. 'And I don't think he despised you... On the contrary, I think he recognised your talent as an artist——'

'How can you say that?' Sally cut in impatiently. Suddenly the suppressed tears were tearing at her throat. 'You heard what he said about my "pathetic little pictures"! That didn't sound like recognition of talent to me!'

'It wasn't meant to. He was trying to hurt you because you'd found him out. But, in fact, I'm sure he thought the opposite.' He held her gaze a moment. 'My theory is that that was one of the main reasons he hooked up with you—so he could exploit your ability as a painter. He probably planned to do with your paintings what he did with the blue owls—flog them off privately under another name.'

'You really think that?' Sally looked back at him. Maybe it was true and maybe it wasn't, but that Josh should say it she found immensely moving.

He nodded. 'I really think it. In fact, I'm quite sure.'

What kind eyes he had. A rush of emotion went through her. No one in the world had kind, compassionate eyes like Josh. 'Thank you,' she whis-

pered. Then she closed her eyes tightly as she felt
a sob rise up in her throat.

And suddenly, she could no longer hold them
back. Hot, helpless tears were pouring down her
face.

'That's better. Let it out. It's not good to hold
it back.' Suddenly, Josh had crossed the short distance between them and was seating himself on the
arm of the sofa, his arms around her, holding her
face against his chest.

'Cry,' he told her, stroking her hair softly. 'Cry
until you're all cried out.'

Sally did, and though the spasm of weeping that
gripped her was intense it was soon over and she
was drying her tears. And Josh was right—she felt
better for it. She no longer felt so tense. She no
longer felt that she might explode.

As she dabbed her cheeks with the handkerchief
he'd produced for her, Josh continued gently to
stroke her hair. 'It'll take you a while to get over
the shock,' he told her. 'But I'm here whenever you
need a shoulder to cry on.' His tone altered slightly.
'It's the very least I can do.'

Sally glanced up at him curiously, slightly be-
mused by the notion of Josh as a shoulder to cry
on. She had thought of him in many ways over the
years she had known him, but never before as a
source of comfort.

She said, 'What do you mean, it's the least you
can do?'

'After what I've accused you of you can still ask
me that?' He smiled a wry smile and smoothed her
hair from her face, his fingers warm and strong,
making her blood tingle. 'Have you forgotten

already that I believed you were a part of all this? Have you forgotten that I believed you were Clive's accomplice?'

In a funny way she had. Sally sighed and shook her head at him. 'What else were you to believe? Considering the way he set me up, it would have been hard for you to believe anything else.'

'Maybe so. But I still owe you an apology. I still have a duty to try and make amends.'

His eyes poured into her, making her shiver. And the remorse there was real and overwhelming. Sally felt the need to tell him, 'As you said, he fooled all of us. I was as close to him as anyone, and he certainly fooled me.'

She paused and pulled a face. 'Well, perhaps that's not quite accurate. Apparently, that other girl was closer to him than I was. You see, I was even wrong about that.'

'I'm really sorry about that. I know how that must hurt.' Josh went on stroking her hair as his eyes poured down on her. 'But you must just try to tell yourself that you've made a lucky escape.'

Sally already knew that. She had passed that hurdle. And it had not been a difficult hurdle to pass.

But she did not say so. Instead, she sighed as she looked back at him. She was thinking how glad she was that Josh was with her. There was no one in the world she'd rather have had with her right now.

'Naturally, the lease on the shop will be renewed. I shall see to that immediately,' Josh was saying. He twisted a loose strand of her hair behind her ear as he continued to gaze down at her through those wondrous jet-black eyes of his. Then he cupped her chin delicately with his fingers. 'Do you think you'll ever be able to forgive me?'

Sally wanted to smile. She wanted to reach out her hand and stroke away the frown that had formed between his brows. She nodded. 'Of course. You made a genuine mistake.'

And it was wonderful to know that, to know that he didn't hate her. For she knew now that, after all, he hadn't acted out of hate. He'd done what he'd done for what had seemed like a very good reason. How could she not forgive him for that?

He was stroking her chin. 'There's still a bit I haven't told you—and you may not find this so easy to forgive... I came here to try and trap you, as well as to close the shop down. I hired someone to keep an eye on Clive—that was how I found out about the girl. But you I'd decided to keep an eye on personally.

'I wanted to keep the police out of it for the reasons I've already told you, because of the respect I have for your parents. It was only this morning when I realised you weren't involved that I got in touch with them and gave them all the details.' He frowned again. 'But, police or no police, I fully intended to extract my pound of flesh.'

'I don't blame you.' Sally meant it. 'I would have felt the same. And you were fifty-per-cent right in your deductions, after all. Clive was guilty enough for both of us.'

'What a girl.' Josh shook his head in stunned admiration. 'I'm glad I didn't mention anything to Aunt Mimi. In spite of what I led you to believe, you'll be glad to hear she knows nothing of what's been going on.'

Sally smiled. 'Yes, I am glad.'

But Josh did not smile back. Instead, his frown simply seemed to grow deeper. 'I really am sorry. I do hope you can forgive me?'

'I forgive you.'

'Truly?'

'Truly. No hard feelings.'

At last, he smiled. 'Let's shake on it,' he said.

'OK, let's shake on it.' Sally held out her hand, feeling a strange warm feeling ripple through her as Josh reached out to take it in his.

And that ought to have been the end of it. A brief handshake and all forgiven. But a moment later they were still seated there on the sofa, hands clasped together, each gazing into the face of the other.

Sally was aware of her heartbeat and of how it had suddenly quickened. She felt a frantic rush of blood in her head. Her lips parted involuntarily. Her head tilted back. Suddenly she was waiting for Josh to kiss her.

He seemed to take forever, still holding her hand tightly, and his dark eyes, all at once filled with fierce emotion, seemed to pierce right through her head. Then, suddenly, when she could bear the waiting no longer, he was drawing her towards him and pressing his lips to hers.

Sally gasped at the shock of it, at the intensity she could sense in him, for this was not the way he had kissed her last time. Before, he had been gentle, exploratory, almost tentative. This time, literally, he took her breath away.

His lips were like a fire consuming her own. His tongue darted hungrily against her teeth. And such

was the force of him that she had no alternative
but to open her mouth wider to grant him access.

He would devour her!

The thought went through her as she responded
with excitement, her tongue colliding with his, impatient and eager. And she longed to be devoured
by him. Her blood was racing. She longed to be
devoured by him, and to devour him in return!

Her arms were round his neck, holding him
tightly, her fingers eagerly twisting in his hair. And
she shivered as, bodily, he moved her along the sofa,
then slid down from the arm into the space
alongside her. Suddenly she was trembling as their
two bodies pressed together.

'Josh! Oh, Josh!'

His name spilled from her lips as he kissed her
face, her chin, her hair. She tugged at his hair, in-
flamed by the thrill of him. 'Oh, Josh, I've waited
so long for this!'

Did she say it out loud? She didn't care if she
had. Recklessly, Sally buried her face against his
neck, repaying kiss with kiss and caress with caress.
In that moment there was nothing in the world for
her but Josh.

'Sally.'

As she fell back against the cushions of the sofa,
drawing him with her, loving the weight of him
against her, a sob broke inside her as he whispered
her name.

Never had she heard a sound so beautiful. Never
had she felt such joy break within her. And she felt
again what she'd felt before—that she'd been
waiting all her life for this.

She pressed her lips to his temple. 'Dear Josh!' she breathed.

His hand was on her breast, caressing, moulding, igniting tongues of fire in her loins. As he strummed her hardening nipple through the cotton of her blouse, she jerked and pressed against him, the breath catching in her throat. 'Oh, Josh,' she murmured. 'I want you so much.'

'And I want you, too. But not here,' he answered. Suddenly, he was rising to his feet and scooping her from the sofa. 'Let's go somewhere a little more comfortable—and private. Roberts could walk in at any moment.'

Then he was carrying her across the room and out into the hall, then down the corridor that led to his bedroom. He pushed the door open and flicked a switch on the wall. With a sigh the curtains closed and a pair of bedside lamps switched on.

'I think this is better.'

The door was locked behind them as he laid her now on the silken bedspread. Then he was bending over her, kissing her face softly. 'Are you sure you really want this?' he said.

'Oh, yes.' She lifted her head and touched her lips to his. 'I think I've wanted it forever.'

He smiled. 'I'd never have guessed.' He lay stomach-down beside her, leaned over her and traced her jawline with his fingertip. Then, as she caught his finger and kissed it, then drew it deep into her mouth, something flared at the back of his eyes again. 'But who am I to disbelieve you?'

As he spoke, with his free hand he had undone the buttons of her blouse. The two sides slipped

apart to reveal her lacy bra. Then as she kissed his
hand, his wrist, his arm, then drew herself up again
to kiss his lips, he had slipped the bra straps from
her shoulders and swept the cups of the bra aside
to release her breasts.

They fell into his hands like two ripe, eager
plums. Softly, he squeezed them, making her shiver.
Then with the flat of his palms he caressed them
unhurriedly, making her blood leap as he bruised
the hardened nipples, circling, strumming, driving
her mad.

'Is this what you've been waiting for?' he
murmured.

'Oh, yes! Yes, Josh!' She was pressing against
him, her hands roaming over him, intoxicated by
the touch of him. 'Oh, yes!' she murmured again,
struggling with his shirt buttons.

A moment later, impatiently, he had torn off his
shirt. It was tossed on the floor along with her
blouse and bra. Then he was leaning over her, a
hungry look in his eye, kissing her lips, her throat,
her shoulders, then, almost savagely, taking hold
of one breast and raising the dark, aching nipple
to his lips.

Sally felt herself very nearly catapult in two at
the shock wave of sensation that went shooting
through her. Suddenly she was on fire, from her
scalp to her toes. And suddenly every throbbing,
heat-filled inch of her was flooded with an aching,
overpowering need.

'Make love to me, Josh,' she whispered against
his hair.

His response was to draw her nipple deeper into
his mouth. She cried out as his teeth gently nibbled

against it. This was excitement, this was pleasure like she'd never even dreamed it—so fierce, so savage, it was almost unbearable.

'Please!'

She couldn't silence the cry that tore from her. I want you! I love you! The words poured through her. I've always wanted you! I've loved you forever!

'Please?'

His voice was gruff as he repeated her plea. He reached for the fastening at the side of her skirt, at the same drawing himself closer against her, so she could feel his hardness burn against her thigh.

A tide of helpless yearning flooded Sally's loins. She closed her eyes and clung to him fiercely. Oh, to feel that hardness that was pressed against her thigh buried deep and strong within her!

And it seemed her desire was about to be fulfilled. Her skirt was undone, the zip pulled down, and the skirt itself on the point of being removed, when suddenly both of them started then instantly froze as the phone on the bedside table began to ring.

For a second neither of them moved. Sally wanted to say, Ignore it. But before she could, Josh was drawing away and reaching out to lift the receiver.

She could see in his eyes that it had crossed his mind just to do as she'd been hoping and switch the phone off. But at the last moment he didn't. He raised it to his ear. 'Hello?' he said. 'Josh Kingsley speaking.'

As he'd reached for the phone, he'd still been leaning over her. One hand was on her breast and he hadn't removed it. But he removed it now as the other party spoke. And suddenly he was moving away from Sally.

'I'll come and pick you up. I'll be as quick as I can.'

As he laid the phone down again, he was rising from the bed. He looked into Sally's face and smiled a lopsided smile. 'I think that was a classic case of saved by the bell.'

Sally felt her heart turn over. A sudden coldness seemed to touch her. A minute ago he'd been so close and now he was as far from her as the dark side of the moon.

She swallowed drily. 'Who was it?' she asked him.

He was bending to pick up his discarded shirt as he answered and didn't see the look of pain that touched her face. Only Sally was aware of the spasm of anguish that tore through her, like some desperate howling demon, as he told her in a calm tone, 'That was Karin. She's at the station. While you get dressed, I'm going to fetch her.'

CHAPTER NINE

AFTER Josh had gone, Sally did what she had to do. She got dressed, combed her hair, collected her bag and left. Half an hour later she was on a train taking her home.

Before she'd left the penthouse, however, she'd scrawled a quick note and left it with Roberts to deliver to Josh.

The message was simple, unambiguous.

> Saved by the bell—you were right about that! Thank heavens it saved us before we did anything we might regret.
>
> I'm going home to lick my wounds and get on with some work. I'll see you around some time. Best wishes, Sally.

As she sat on the train on the hour-long journey home, she repeated the brief message over in her head. She felt it struck the right note. It renewed the distance between them without being unnecessarily cold or aggressive. And that was what she wanted. To keep Josh at a distance. To have him believe she cared nothing for him at all.

Through the tears that filled her eyes the moving landscape was a blur. If only it were true, that she really felt that way. But she didn't, not any more. And perhaps she never had.

Sally swallowed, trying to shift the tightness in her throat. But it would not budge. It was lodged there like a stone. And it grew more unbearable each time she thought of Josh.

I love him, her mind kept repeating, over and over. I love him more than I love my own life. And I've always loved him. He's always been a part of me. Only, until today, I was unable to face the truth.

She had wondered at first if the whole notion was crazy. Perhaps these feelings were simply a delusion that had somehow sprung out of the emotional trauma of the discovery of her cruel betrayal by Clive. Perhaps they were simply a hysterical reaction.

She almost wished they were, that they could be so easily explained away. But she knew that wasn't so. There had been no emotional trauma. All there had been, regarding Clive, was anger and disappointment. And something else, she had realised a little to her own shame—a sense of liberation from a false emotional bond.

There had never been more than friendship between her and Clive; and even that, if she was honest, had never gone very deep. She had certainly never loved him and she had never seriously considered marrying him. She'd been drawn into the relationship because it had seemed to please Clive. And because it had seemed harmless. That was the plain, simple truth.

She frowned to herself. And Clive, it now seemed, had pursued the relationship for monetary gain. Perhaps he'd proposed marriage in the hope of taking over the shop, or to take control of the sale of her paintings, as Josh had suggested. And all the while, with his blonde accomplice, he'd been leading a double life—and had been intending to continue doing so, no doubt.

Sally shook her head inwardly. What a fool I was, she was thinking, ever to have got mixed up with Clive in the first place. But the thought was not painful. It merely irked her. No, as regards Clive, she had suffered no emotional trauma.

But as to Josh . . . That was different. She felt the tightness in her throat grow tighter. The hot tears that blurred her eyes threatened to spill over. What had happened between her and Josh had seared her soul for life.

She felt her heart twist inside her as she remembered how he had kissed her. How he had kissed her and carried her through to his bedroom, then gone on kissing her and very nearly made love to her. And how she, without inhibition, without shame, had responded. Even now the longing leapt in her at the memory of his touch.

She had thought then—and she'd even told him!—that she'd waited all her life for this. To feel his kiss, his warm embrace, his passionate possession. But these thoughts and words had held a far deeper truth.

To feel him hold her and kiss her, that was a part of what she'd longed for, but the real moment of truth had been the unleashing inside her of all the love she felt for him and had for so long suppressed. Suddenly, she'd no longer felt the need to deny it. It had swept through her like a hurricane, uplifting her soul.

In that moment when she'd realised that she loved him, it had felt like letting go, like a release of warmth within her. It had felt like shaking off a

long-held, crippling fear. And, briefly, she had
exulted in this warm, new feeling, filled with the
joy of it, full of hope and optimism.

But her joy had been brief.

For then the phone had rung.

Sally smiled a wry smile. She had forgotten about
Karin. The ubiquitous Karin, who was so helpless,
it now seemed, that not only did she rush to Josh
with all her problems, but she wasn't even capable
of taking a taxi from the station! She had to phone
Josh and wheedle a lift!

But perhaps it was just as well that she had. Sally
took a deep breath. There was no point in being
bitchy about Karin. How would it have looked if
Karin had turned up at the penthouse to find her
lover in bed with Sally?

Bad, she decided. Bad for Karin. From her own
point of view, she suspected, it might have felt
rather good!

Sally pressed back in her seat and breathed deeply
for a moment. She was only thinking these flippant
thoughts to stop herself from weeping. For she
knew it would have changed nothing if she'd been
caught in bed with Josh. Nothing essential. He still
wouldn't love her.

What was it he'd said to her? 'I still have a duty
to try and make amends.' That was why he'd been
so kind to her, why he'd consoled her with his
kisses—because he'd sensed she wanted it and he
had felt he owed it to her.

It was a shattering thought, but Sally sensed it
was the truth.

A sudden jolt told her the train had reached her station. She rose to her feet stiffly and headed for the door.

So what's changed? she told herself as she hurried through the ticket barrier, then outside into the street to catch a taxi. Surely nothing in my life that really matters? I still have my business. I still have my painting. Clive's gone, but that's a plus, not a minus. And, as far as Josh and I are concerned, nothing has changed.

She hailed a taxi and climbed into the rear seat. 'The High Street,' she told the driver. 'Dovecote Flats.'

So what's the problem? she demanded of herself, as the taxi set off. All I have to do is carry on as before.

Sally stared out of the window, blinking fiercely, holding on tightly to the bag in her lap. For in her heart she knew that everything had changed, so how could she carry on as before?

She bit her lip to smother a shiver of pain. For she knew the question she really ought to be asking herself was, where would she find the strength to carry on at all when her heart lay broken like a pane of glass inside her, scattering splinters that tore apart her very soul?

'I'd like you to take over the running of the shop in the meantime. I know you can do it. I know you'll do a great job.'

Sharon's eyes had widened to a pair of bright blue saucers. 'Do you really mean that, Sally? I'm thrilled! I can't believe it! And I won't let you down. I promise you that.'

'I know you won't.' Sally smiled at her kindly. 'I have every confidence in your capabilities.'

It was after hours at the shop and the two girls were seated at the counter, chatting over a cup of coffee.

Sharon glanced across at Sally. 'This really means a lot to me. As you know, I still haven't been able to find a job, and it's not easy surviving on part-time wages——' She broke off and frowned. 'I hope you're not just offering me this chance as a favour? I can manage. There's really no need for you to do that.'

Sally frowned back at her mock seriously. Then she laughed and reassured her, 'Of course not, silly! I'm doing it because of the reason I told you—so I can devote more of my time to painting. And because I need someone I can trust to look after the shop and I couldn't think of anyone more suitable than you.' She squeezed Sharon's arm. '*You're* doing *me* a favour.'

Sharon smiled, reassured, and took a mouthful of her coffee. Then she regarded Sally almost guiltily over the top of her cup. 'I don't want to sound ungrateful, but I think I have to tell you——'

But, before she could finish, Sally cut in, 'I know what you're going to say... that you're still hoping to find a job in computers, that you don't regard this as a long-term thing. That's OK, Sharon. I understand that.' She smiled wryly. 'And I hope you find a job soon, even though it'll mean me having to find someone else—that is, if I decide to carry on with the shop.'

Sharon looked at her admiringly. 'Are you really serious, then, about making your painting a full-time thing? I think that's marvellous. After all, you're so talented it seems a shame for you to do anything else.'

'Thanks for the vote of confidence.' Sally stifled a flush of pleasure. 'It's what I've always wanted and I've decided the time is right now—at least, it will be if I can sell a few more paintings! I'm going to give myself six months, and see how things stand then. By then I ought to be in a position to make some sort of decision.'

'Oh, I'm sure it'll work out for you!' Sharon beamed at her delightedly. 'After all, you sold those last two paintings with no bother at all. I'll bet in six months' time buyers will be queueing up at your front door!'

What a very pleasant thought! The stuff that dreams were made on!

Sally laughed. 'That would be nice, but in the meantime I'd happily settle for just knowing that I can sell enough to make painting my full-time job.'

With a brisk smile she stood up. 'So, I'd better get cracking. I'll never do it if I sit here chatting!' She drained her coffee-cup. 'It's time I got down to some work. That masterpiece in my studio isn't going to paint itself!'

'That's right. Off you go! I'll lock up tonight.' Sharon gathered up the coffee-cups and headed for the back room. 'You go on home and get on with what you're good at. But don't work too late.' She threw Sally a frown across her shoulder. 'My dad said that when he passed your flat after midnight the other night the light was still burning in your studio. Dedication's very well, but you don't want to overdo it.'

'Don't worry, I won't.' Sally smiled at her concern as she swung her brown leather bag over her shoulder. 'It's just that I get most of my inspiration after midnight.' She winked at Sharon teasingly. 'You know how we artists are.' Then she was heading for the door. 'I'll see you tomorrow. Thanks for locking up. Goodnight.'

But outside, as she headed home, Sally felt her brightness fade. Suddenly sadness tugged inside her. What was it she'd said—that she got most of her inspiration after midnight? That had been a deliberate cover-up. After midnight was when thoughts of Josh came to torment her. And working till she dropped was the only way to drive them out.

She set her jaw and plunged her hands into her jacket pockets as she headed down the street towards Dovecote Flats. Nearly a month had passed since she'd last seen Josh, or heard from him, or had any news at all. Since he'd walked out of his bedroom door to go and pick up Karin it was as though he'd vanished off the face of the earth.

It was for the best, Sally told herself, as at last she reached the flats. She couldn't have borne to set eyes on him again. What would she have to say to him? Or he to her? No, it was better that he should stay out of her way.

And her sadness would pass. She knew it would. Eventually. In time this pain that throbbed and tore inside her would recede to become no more than a dull ache, an ache that she was barely even aware of any more.

And then she would be released. No longer would she be driven to remain at her easel until she had no more strength to stand, until the paintbrush was literally dropping from her fingers, and she knew that, at last, it was safe to go to bed, that the demons couldn't touch her, that she had not the strength to weep.

She slipped her key into the lock. Yes, that day would come. That day when there were no more tears and no more hoping. No more dreaming dreams that could never come true.

But not yet. Not tonight. For tonight the pain was fierce, pressing like a spike-knuckled fist within her breast.

She pushed the door open and headed for her studio. Tonight was going to be another long night.

It was two days later, Sunday at last, and the painting Sally was working on was in its final stages.

She'd been working on it since morning, after a surprisingly good night's sleep, the best night's sleep she'd had for weeks. I've come to terms with things, she'd decided earlier over her cornflakes. The worst is over. I'm back in control again. I've put Josh where he should be, out of my head and out of my life.

It was a liberating thought. She'd set about her painting with renewed vigour. If I can forget Josh, I can do anything. Nothing can stop me.

Sally smiled to herself now as she mixed fresh colours with her palette knife. Perhaps, later, for a change, she might go for a walk and drop in on some friends for a chat and a coffee. That would do her good. She'd been working so hard lately.

Obsessively, really. More than was healthy. A bit of amiable socialising would provide a welcome break. She dabbed colour on her paintbrush and turned back to her canvas. She felt better already. More human again.

But it was at that precise moment, as she stood there, paintbrush poised, that suddenly the front doorbell rang.

Sally paused and turned around, then smiled to herself, remembering. That'll be Sharon, she decided. Sharon had said she'd drop round with the greetings card samples that someone had brought into the shop yesterday to show her.

'The door's open!' she called. 'I'm in the studio!'

The door opened as she leaned forward and dabbed colour on to the canvas, and she could hear footsteps approaching down the hall. 'Just lay them down somewhere. I'll look at them later.' Then she turned round with a smile. 'So how are you this morning?'

And that was when her heart slammed hard against her ribs, knocking the breath from her body, rendering her speechless. As she stood staring into his face, the paintbrush dropped from her fingers.

Josh stepped forward. 'I'm fine, thanks,' he answered. Then with a smile he bent down to retrieve the paintbrush. 'Here,' he said. 'You seem to have dropped this.'

'Thanks.'

Sally took it numbly. Her blood was clattering inside her. What was it she'd been thinking earlier? That she'd finally got over him? That she'd expelled him from her head and from her life? Delight and sadness flooded through her now as she gazed up helplessly into his face. She'd been fooling herself. She still loved him with all her heart.

She swallowed. 'Why have you come?' She wanted to reach out and touch him. Suddenly she longed to spill out everything.

And as she waited for him to answer, her eyes searched deep into his. Dared she hope that this visit might be the answer to her dreams?

But then he spoke. 'We've come to extend an apology. A belated apology, but sincere none the less...'

We? The sound of the word was like a cold finger laid on her. Sally felt herself stiffen. Her eyes flickered from his face, as suddenly in the doorway she was aware of a movement. Over his shoulder she could see Karin stepping into the room.

'Sally...' With a small frown Karin was heading towards her. 'I wanted to come before... as soon as I knew... but I've been tied up over the past few weeks in France. I thought about writing or phoning, but I wanted to speak to you in person...'

She paused and smiled an embarrassed, apologetic smile. 'What I'm trying to say is that I'm really sorry for the way I was so rude to you before. Ignoring you the way I did... Refusing to speak to you...' She bit her lip and sighed. 'I'm really ashamed of that.'

Sally was having difficulty standing. Her legs had turned to water. So, the romance between Josh and Karin was still flourishing. So much for her own brief, foolish hope that her secret dreams were about to come true!

But she had known that hope was foolish. All Josh would ever feel for her was at best a kind of friendship, and at worst, and far more likely, no more than sympathy and guilt.

She swallowed drily and forced her eyes to fix on Karin. 'Don't worry,' she told her. 'I understand. The way things stood it was only natural for you to be angry with me.'

'I'm really sorry. Do you forgive me?' Karin held out her hand. 'I won't rest until you do.'

'You're forgiven.' Distractedly, Sally reached out to take her hand, but suddenly Josh was catching her by the arm.

He was smiling. He said, 'You've forgotten about the paintbrush.'

'Oh, yes. The paintbrush.' He was absolutely right. Sally had quite forgotten it was still in her hand. As she met his smiling eyes she could feel her heart weeping. The touch of his hand against her arm was unbearable.

But instantly he had released her. She laid the brush on the table, taking a deep silent breath, pulling herself together. And then, with a forced smile, she shook Karin's hand.

'Don't worry about it,' she told the other girl. 'There's really nothing to forgive.'

Karin clasped her hand gratefully. 'I should have known,' she told her. 'I've known you since both of us were kids. I ought to have known that you were innocent, that you weren't capable of doing such a thing.'

'There are many things about Sally that we all ought to have known.'

As Josh spoke, Sally glanced at him, then glanced away quickly, barely aware of what he was saying. All she knew was that his closeness was choking the life out of her. She wanted him to leave, but she knew she couldn't have borne that either.

'I hear Clive's been charged and will come to trial soon.'

It was a relief when Karin spoke again. Sally fixed her gaze gratefully on her face. 'Yes,' she observed. 'That's good news indeed.' She smiled. 'I hope you manage to get back some of the money he stole from you.'

'That would be nice.' Karin nodded. 'But the main thing is that his little game's been stopped— and I can finally start selling my work under my own name.'

Then she glanced at her watch. 'Hey, time to go! I didn't realise it was this late.' She smiled at Sally. 'Sorry again. And thanks for accepting my apologies. I really do mean them from the bottom of my heart.'

'As I said, that's OK.' The words felt like bricks in her mouth. As Karin started to turn to leave, only one thought was in Sally's head. Was this it? Was Josh about to leave, too?

It certainly looked as though that was Karin's intention. She laid a hand on Josh's sleeve as though about to lead him off with her. But then she said, 'I'll see you later, Josh—and you too, I hope, Sally.'

'Of course.' Sally nodded. Suddenly her heart had started beating again. He wasn't going. Not just yet. She felt her blood suddenly flow warm again.

Neither spoke until the front door had closed behind Karin. Then Josh stepped away a little, widening the distance between them. He leaned his hips against the wooden table where Sally kept her paints and things and surveyed her for a moment with an oddly shuttered look.

Then he said, 'Aunt Mimi's solicitor tells me you've taken an option on the lease, allowing you to terminate it at any time.'

'Yes, that's right.' It was still hard to look at him. Every time she met his eyes something deep inside her seemed to flare up and die in the very same instant. To see him was such joy, but at the same time such agony.

She took a deep breath. 'As you probably know, when they sent me the lease-renewal papers to sign I warned them that I might not want to keep the shop on for long. So they put in an option allowing me to terminate the lease at one month's notice whenever I wish.'

'Yes, so they told me.' He was still watching her closely, the dark eyes narrowed, his expression careful. 'I hope your reasons for doing that were not negative ones?'

Sally frowned, not quite certain she understood what he meant. 'Negative—in what way?' she demanded.

Josh shrugged. 'I hope you're not planning on running away. People sometimes feel the urge to do that after they've had an unpleasant experience like the one you've had. You know...leave it all behind, make a fresh start...'

Yes, she'd been right. Sympathy and guilt—they were the only feelings he had for her. She made an effort to smother the wretched way that made her feel.

Sally shook her head. She didn't want his guilt and sympathy. She said in a clear tone, 'No, that's not the reason. I just want to have a go at being a painter full-time. At least, I want to in six months' time if it looks as if it might be viable. I don't want to burn my bridges until I'm sure.'

'I wouldn't worry about burning bridges. You can make it. I'm sure of it.' As he spoke, Josh detached himself from the table and stepped towards her, studying the canvas at her back. 'I'd say there's no doubt about it, if this is anything to go by.'

'Thanks.' In spite of herself, Sally flushed with pleasure. 'It's still not quite finished, but I'm nearly there.'

'I like it.' He was still studying it. 'Do you have a buyer?'

'A potential buyer. He has first refusal. He recently bought a couple of other paintings of mine.' As Josh turned to look at her, she hurried on in sudden confusion, her nerves tingling at the way he was standing so close to her, 'You see, I've already started selling.'

'Yes, I know.' There was a strange look in his eyes. There was something he wasn't saying, something he was holding back. Suddenly Sally could sense it very strongly.

She looked up into his face. 'I'm surprised,' she said.

'Why? I may have been out of the country, but I haven't been completely out of touch. One gets to hear about such things.'

'Does one?'

For an instant she had to look away. So, he'd been out of the country. At least that explained one thing—who it was Karin had been tied up with in France. Not that it mattered *where* they'd been. What hurt was that they'd been together, and she'd already guessed that.

She looked back at him again, trying to thrust aside her folly. And she could see it there still, that look in his eyes, oddly guarded, hiding something.

He was saying as he turned once more to glance at the painting, 'I'm sure you'll sell this one as easily as the others. This buyer of yours...I can't see him saying no. In fact I'm sure he'll snap it up.'

'Why are you so sure?' A sudden fear had struck her. She clenched her fists, eyes fixed on the back of his neck. 'Why are you so sure?' she said again, tightly.

'Because it's good. Damned good, in my opinion.'

But he still wasn't looking at her, and the more he didn't look, the more firm in her mind Sally's suspicion was becoming.

It was Josh who had bought her paintings! He was the unknown buyer! And he had done it out of remorse, in order to make amends to her!

The thought was unbearable. It jolted her out of her stupor. Suddenly she was reaching out and taking hold of his sleeve and tugging him round to look straight at her.

'What aren't you telling me? It's about the paintings, isn't it? Well, I think you should come clean! I have a right to know!'

His eyes were on her then. For an instant he frowned down at her. Then, to her utter astonishment, he was taking hold of her. '*You're* the one who should come clean!' he railed at her. '*I'm* the one who has a right to know!'

Sally was frozen in his grip, her heart rushing inside her. 'I don't know what you mean!' His eyes were like firebrands, scorching right down to the roots of her soul. 'I have nothing to come clean about! You're the one who's hiding something!'

'Hiding something?' He shook her impatiently. 'You're the one who hides things! You can hide the truth for years!'

'What truth?' She was bewildered. What was he so upset about? Because he *was* upset. Through the impatience that poured from him she could see that something was scraping at his heart. 'What truth?' she demanded again. 'What are you talking about?'

Josh took a deep breath, as though to still his emotions. His grip on her arms was firm and tight. Then he said with a sigh, 'I'm talking about the necklace. That necklace of Aunt Mimi's that you've allowed me to go on believing you tried to steal all those years ago...' He snatched a breath and shook her gently. 'I know now that you never tried to steal it.'

Sally looked at him, wide-eyed. Where on earth had this sprung from? She'd been in the midst of accusing him of secretly buying her paintings, and suddenly he was talking about Aunt Mimi's necklace!

But as he shook her again, demanding some response, she admitted, 'No, of course I never tried to steal it.'

Josh nodded. 'Karin told me. Last night at my flat we were talking about you and what a rough deal we've given you... and as we were talking she

remembered the story Lucinda told her years
ago... the story about how she set you up with the
necklace and made it look as though you'd tried to
steal it...'

'Lucinda told her that?'

'Years ago, apparently. Lucinda thought the
whole thing was a tremendous joke.' He shook his
head. 'Karin thought nothing about it at the time.
She had no idea,' he added sombrely, 'that for years
that incident had soured my feelings towards you.'

Sally felt herself flush at the regret in his voice.
But she forced herself to say, 'Surely "soured" is
a bit strong? You may not always have believed I
was a thief, but the truth is, you never really liked
me much anyway.'

Josh's eyebrows rose at that. 'Of course I liked
you. Why on earth would you say a thing like that?'

'It was just a feeling I had.' She looked at him
curiously. Was that really shock she could see in
his eyes?

He certainly sounded shocked. 'Then you were
crazy! If that's what you believed, it was all in your
head! I didn't just *like* you, to me you were almost
a part of the family! Why else,' he put to her,
'would I have kept that photograph of you and me
and Aunt Mimi all those years?' He looked into
her eyes. 'You know the photograph I'm talking
about?'

Sally swallowed and nodded. 'The one in your
flat in the silver frame.'

So, she was thinking, her inclusion in the photograph had not been an oversight, after all. She bit
her lip and glanced away quickly, blushing bright
crimson with happiness and confusion.

'I don't know why I thought it—probably just childish insecurity,' she added, 'but I really did think you didn't like me all that much.'

'Well, I have to say you were the only one who thought it! The other girlfriends I used to bring round were all terribly jealous of you. Especially Lucinda, now that I come to think of it. She thought I was much too fond of you.'

'Lucinda was jealous of *me*?' The very notion astonished her. Without thinking, she found herself blurting out, 'I was the one who was jealous of her!'

It was the first time she'd really admitted it, even to herself. All of that so-called disapproval of hers had really been jealousy! But she wished with all her heart that she hadn't said it.

Mortified by her indiscretion, Sally stared at the floor, wishing with all her strength that it might swallow her up.

And she felt sure Josh must be laughing at her as he answered, 'I feel flattered.'

There was a pause. Sally continued to stare at the floor. Then he released one of her arms, took hold of her chin and gently raised her face to force her to look at him.

'Why didn't you tell me years ago about the necklace?' he demanded.

'I didn't think it mattered.' She was finding it hard to look at him. She had expected him to be smiling at her mockingly, but he wasn't.

'You didn't think it mattered, because I didn't like you anyway?' His eyes were pouring into her, giving her goosebumps. A frown touched his brow. 'Is that what you're saying?'

'Yes. I suppose so.' But she realised now that there had been another, more devious reason as well. She had used the misunderstanding to keep a distance between them. She had been afraid, for her heart's sake, of getting too close to him. For, even way back then, she had loved him.

'I wish I'd known. I wish I'd known years ago.' Josh sighed. 'Perhaps if I'd known the truth about the necklace I wouldn't have been so easily persuaded that you were a part of this business with Clive.' He released her suddenly, stood back and looked at her. 'What a lot of years you and I have wasted.'

'Wasted?' What was he saying? Suddenly her heart was skipping. Sally tried to douse the feeling. She said, 'We could have been friends.'

'Yes, we could.' He continued to watch her. 'But in the end it didn't matter.'

The skipping stopped. Sally's heart lurched inside her. She said flatly, 'No, of course not. It didn't matter.'

There was a pause. Sally could hear his breathing as he watched her. Then he said, 'Do you know where I've been for the past few weeks?'

Sally was about to say no, then suddenly she remembered. And the memory was like a fist to her solar plexus. Stiff-faced, she answered, 'With Karin. In France.'

'What? With Karin? What would I be doing with Karin?'

'I don't know... What people do... I mean, she *is* your girlfriend...'

'My *what*?' Suddenly, Josh was taking hold of her and laughing. 'So that's what you've been thinking? I don't believe it!' he exclaimed.

'Of course it's what I've been thinking. Why are you so surprised?'

'Because Karin's never been my girlfriend!' He shook her gently. 'You crazy girl. Karin and I are just friends! And we've never been anything more than just friends!'

Sally stared at him, bewildered, wondering if she dared believe him. She said, dry-mouthed, 'So what have you been doing?'

To add to her bewilderment, Josh bent down and kissed her nose. 'What I've been doing is having meetings with all my overseas connections, organising things so I need spend less time abroad.'

He paused and looked down at her, his expression suddenly serious. 'Do you want to know why I've been doing that?' he asked her.

Sally nodded, still half dazed by her sense of bewilderment. Those times she'd seen Karin at the mansion, she was thinking, nothing had been going on, after all. Suddenly, anxiously, her heart was beating.

Josh continued to hold her as he went on to explain to her, 'I know from experience that the sort of life I've been leading—rushing all over the globe all the time—is OK for a single man, but not for a man with a wife and family. And that's why I've decided to make some changes...'

He took a deep breath. 'I'm not trying to rush you. I know I still have to woo and win you...and I know you still have to finish getting over Clive.

But I think I should warn you, I want to marry you, Sally...'

'Marry me?' She had to hold on to him to stop herself from falling. Her hands were on his arms, clutching on tightly.

'You don't have to think about it yet... As I said, I won't rush you——' Then he broke off, his eyes clouding, as she began to shake her head.

'No, Josh, you're wrong.' Suddenly that dazed feeling had gone. Suddenly everything seemed simple and clear and bright, and she could feel her heart thumping like a wild thing inside her. Sally shook her head. 'I don't have to get over Clive. Clive was a mistake. I was never in love with him. The only man I've ever been in love with is you.'

'Do you mean that?' The eyes that just a moment ago had been clouded were suddenly beaming at her with astonished delight. 'And I've always loved you. I didn't fully realise it until that day we almost made love at my flat. I decided then I was going to marry you—in spite of that discouraging little note you left me.'

He smiled and kissed her nose again. 'It was that note that made me decide you probably needed some time—to get over Clive and all the rest——'

'That wasn't why I wrote the note.' Sally smiled and leaned against him, winding her arms around his neck. 'I wrote it because I suddenly knew I loved you—and I thought that you were involved with Karin.'

'What a crazy pair we are!' Suddenly Josh was laughing and lifting her bodily up into his arms. 'Let's go somewhere quiet, lock the door behind us, take the phone off the hook and spend the next

couple of years sorting out all this dreadful muddle
we've created and getting to know each other
properly.' He bent and kissed her face. 'Which way
to the bedroom?'

Sally kissed him back, her heart swelling inside
her. Could all this really be happening? It was too
much to take in.

'First things first,' she told him. 'Was it you who
bought my paintings? I have to know. I have to
know the truth.'

Josh frowned, then understood. 'So that's what
you were on about.' He shook his head. 'No, I
didn't buy your paintings. Nor do I know who
bought them—but I do know he has good taste.'

As she smiled with relief, he continued, 'So,
answer my question. Which way to the bedroom,
Mrs Kingsley-to-be?'

'That way,' Sally pointed, then reached up to kiss
his chin. 'What makes you so sure I'm going to be
Mrs Kingsley?'

'Because I won't give up until you say yes.' He
was heading for the bedroom, carrying her in his
arms. 'If I have to ask you a thousand million times
I won't give up until you agree. And I'll use a
thousand million kisses to persuade you.'

'You make holding out sound tempting.'

'Not that tempting. I won't make love to you even
once until you say yes.'

'Ah.'

'So, will you marry me?' He laid her on the bed.

Sally sighed and, kissing him, drew him down
beside her, suddenly filled with more happiness than
she had ever dreamed of. What choice did she have?

'Yes,' she said.

*   *   *

Less than two months later, in her Regent's Park studio, Mrs Josh Kingsley regarded the portrait she was working on—a bold head-and-shoulders portrait of her husband—and smiled a smile of deep satisfaction.

In a matter of weeks, Sally's whole life had changed. She'd given up the shop—Sharon had found a job!—and she'd moved to London after a lavish wedding, for which the entire village had turned out and at which Aunt Mimi had been guest of honour. And she'd never been happier in her life.

She blew the painting a kiss, then suddenly sighed, laid down her paintbrush and slipped off her smock. What was she doing throwing kisses at a painting when the flesh-and-blood subject of the painting was waiting for her?

Two minutes later she stepped into the bedroom where Josh, newly showered, was waiting for her in bed, looking even more spectacular, even more deeply tanned, after their three-week honeymoon in Florida.

'At last,' he said, leaning against the pillows and smiling at her.

Sally felt her heart turn over. 'I've almost finished with you,' she said. Then she smiled and pulled a face. 'I mean the painting.'

He smiled back at her and reached for her. 'Well, I haven't nearly finished with you.' He kissed her. 'In fact, I haven't even started with you yet.'

Sally kissed him back, feeling her flesh melt at the touch of him. 'As soon as I've finished that one I'm going to do another one. I'll never find a better subject than you.'

'And as soon as I've finished making love to you I'm going to make love to you all over again. I'll never find another woman I want as much as you.'

'So this could take some time, then?'

Josh smiled. 'A lifetime.'

Sally sank blissfully into his arms. 'That's rather what I was hoping.'

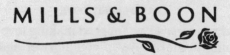

MILLS & BOON

EXCITING NEW COVERS

To reflect the ever-changing contemporary romance series we've designed new covers which perfectly capture the warmth, glamour and sophistication of modern-day romantic situations.

We know, because we've designed them with your comments in mind, that you'll just love the bright, warm, romantic colours and the up-to-date new look.

WATCH OUT FOR THESE NEW COVERS

From October 1993   Price £1.80

*Available from W.H. Smith, John Menzies, Martins, Forbuoys, most supermarkets and other paperback stockists.
Also available from Mills & Boon Reader Service, Freepost, PO Box 236, Thornton Road, Croydon, Surrey CR9 9EL. (UK Postage & Packing free)*

Mills & Boon

Proudly present to you...

BETTY NEELS' 100TH ROMANCE

Betty has been writing for Mills & Boon Romances for over 20 years. She began once she had retired from her job as a Ward Sister. She is married to a Dutchman and spent many years in Holland. Both her experiences as a nurse and her knowledge and love of Holland feature in many of her novels.

Her latest romance *'AT ODDS WITH LOVE'* is available from August 1993, price £1.80.

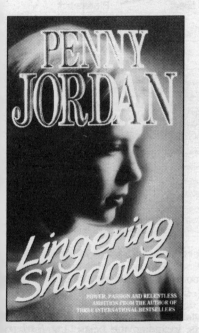

Next Month's Romances

Each month you can choose from a wide variety of romance with Mills & Boon. Below are the new titles to look out for next month, why not ask either Mills & Boon Reader Service or your Newsagent to reserve you a copy of the titles you want to buy – just tick the titles you would like and either post to Reader Service or take it to any Newsagent and ask them to order your books.

Please save me the following titles:	Please tick	√
THE WEDDING	Emma Darcy	
LOVE WITHOUT REASON	Alison Fraser	
FIRE IN THE BLOOD	Charlotte Lamb	
GIVE A MAN A BAD NAME	Roberta Leigh	
TRAVELLING LIGHT	Sandra Field	
A HEALING FIRE	Patricia Wilson	
AN OLD ENCHANTMENT	Amanda Browning	
STRANGERS BY DAY	Vanessa Grant	
CONSPIRACY OF LOVE	Stephanie Howard	
FIERY ATTRACTION	Emma Richmond	
RESCUED	Rachel Elliot	
DEFIANT LOVE	Jessica Hart	
BOGUS BRIDE	Elizabeth Duke	
ONE SHINING SUMMER	Quinn Wilder	
TRUST TOO MUCH	Jayne Bauling	
A TRUE MARRIAGE	Lucy Gordon	

If you would like to order these books in addition to your regular subscription from Mills & Boon Reader Service please send £1.80 per title to: Mills & Boon Reader Service, Freepost, P.O. Box 236, Croydon, Surrey, CR9 9EL, quote your Subscriber No:.................................. (If applicable) and complete the name and address details below. Alternatively, these books are available from many local Newsagents including W.H.Smith, J.Menzies, Martins and other paperback stockists from 10 September 1993.

Name:...

Address:..

....Post Code:...........................

To Retailer: If you would like to stock M&B books please contact your regular book/magazine wholesaler for details.

You may be mailed with offers from other reputable companies as a result of this application. If you would rather not take advantage of these opportunities please tick box ☐